ABOUT THIS BOOK

The Computer Nut
BETSY BYARS

When Kate receives a message on her computer from a mysterious admirer, she hopes it's her secret crush, Willie Lomax. Willie just might be crazy enough to pretend he's BB-9, an alien comedian in search of a good laugh (he does look a little like BB-9's self-portrait, a pear wearing a lampshade). But Kate gets discouraged when no one wants to help her solve the biggest mystery-romance of her life. Her parents don't want her involved with any computer weirdos (especially extraterrestrial ones), her dizzy sister is too busy planning a dogs' birthday party, and only her best friend, Linda, is eager to help—with a wide range of sure-to-backfire schemes. Surviving Linda's plot, Willie does prove he's innocent—and a good sport about an "accidental" flea-dip bath. He also proves he's a resourceful computer sleuth when he teams up with Kate for a hilarious close encounter with the alien comedian.

Also by Betsy Byars

After the Goat Man
The Cartoonist
Cracker Jackson
The Cybil War
The 18th Emergency
The Glory Girl
Go and Hush the Baby
The House of Wings
The Midnight Fox
The Summer of the Swans
Trouble River
The TV Kid
The Winged Colt of Casa Mia

The Computer Nut

BETSY BYARS

Computer Graphics by Guy Byars

SCHOLASTIC INC.
New York Toronto London Auckland Sydney

To Guy, with love

Copyright © 1984 by Betsy Byars.
Cover illustration copyright © 1991 by Scott Gladden.
All rights reserved. Published by Scholastic Inc., 730 Broadway, New York, NY 10003, by arrangement with Viking Penguin, a division of Penguin Books USA Inc.
Printed in the U.S.A.
ISBN 0-590-46521-X

2 3 4 5 6 7 8 9 10   40   99 98 97 96 95 94 93

Contents

The Computer Nut

Self-Portrait of a Computer Nut

Kate was drawing a picture of herself on her father's computer. She had been working for an hour. She was half finished when Miss Markham came and stood in the doorway behind her.

"I'm ready to close the office now, Kate," she said.

Kate flicked her hair behind her ears. She did not answer. She continued to turn the thumbwheels, drawing lines between the dots. Her eyes watched the screen intently.

"Kate, did you hear me? The last patient has left. Your father has gone to the hospital. I'm ready to close the office now."

"Go ahead. I'll lock the doors when I leave."

"You know that's against your father's orders."

"Well, I've *got* to finish this. It's homework and it's due tomorrow."

"Katie—"

"Miss Markham, this is the first art assignment I've ever been interested in. Last week you know what we did? We made Indian signs out of yarn, and before that we pasted macaroni on cardboard. Now, *finally,* we are doing something I'm interested in, and I've got to finish."

Miss Markham crossed the room and stood behind Kate. She watched the screen as Kate connected the dots for her mouth. "That does *not* look like homework."

"It is! Our assignment is to do a self-portrait."

"On a computer?"

"No. We're supposed to use our imaginations. Willie Lomax is doing a collage out of candy wrappers. His freckles are M & M's. He's calling it Sweet Freak."

"What are you calling yours?"

"Self-Portrait of a Computer Nut."

"Good title."

"I like it." Kate smiled without glancing around.

Miss Markham watched as Kate drew circles in her eyes. She sighed. "All right, Kate, you can keep working until I change out of my uniform."

"Thanks."

"But then you have *got* to leave whether you're through or not."

"I'll be through."

As Miss Markham started for the door, she added, "If you're not, you'll have to call it 'Unfinished Portrait of a Computer Nut.' Ten minutes, Kate."

"Right."

With her eyes watching the screen, Kate drew the straight lines for her hair. She paused to look at what she'd done. "Not bad." She typed "Self-Portrait of a Computer Nut" beneath the picture. Then she pushed the button marked "Hard Copy" and waited while the machine printed the picture.

When the sheet of paper slid out the side, Kate picked it up. "That does look like me," she said to herself.

She turned to shut off the computer and saw Miss Markham in the doorway. "Perfect timing," Kate said. She held up her picture. "What do you think?"

"Not bad. Your hair's never that neat, though."

"I know, and I also have more freckles, and braces on my teeth."

She eyed the sheet of paper critically. "Well, it's better than Willie's candy portrait. You know what happened last summer? I meant to tell you this. Willie went to the same computer camp I did, and when we were checking in, his suitcase fell open, and there was a real thin layer of clothes—one T-shirt and a pair of socks—and the whole rest of the suitcase was junk food. He had enough Snickers to—"

"Kate, I have not got time to talk about Willie Lomax."

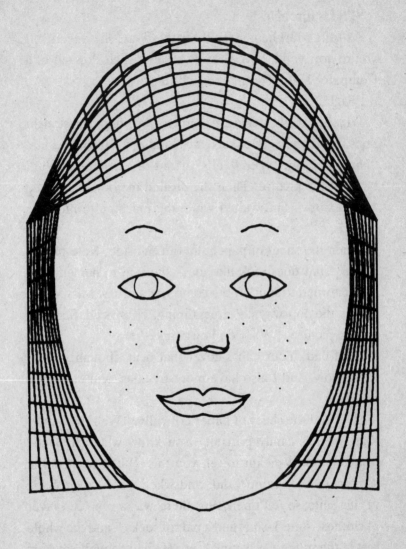

"I don't want to talk about him either!" Kate said quickly. She turned back to the computer to hide her expression. "I just wanted you to know that next time he's in for a checkup do not believe him when he says he has stuck to his diet."

Kate slipped out the disk containing the drawing program. To change the subject, she said, "Where are you going, Miss Markham? Do you have a date?"

"Not unless I leave right this minute."

"I'm coming! I'm coming!"

Kate was reaching for the off button when suddenly words began appearing on the video screen. She stopped, her hand frozen in midair.

"That's crazy!"

She glanced at the door to see if Miss Markham had noticed, but Miss Markham was in the outer office, turning off the lights. Kate sank into the chair, her portrait forgotten in her lap.

The words on the CRT screen were:

> I HAVE JUST SEEN THE PORTRAIT OF THE COM-
> PUTER NUT AND I WOULD LIKE TO MAKE CON-
> TACT. WILL YOU RECEIVE A MESSAGE,
> COMPUTER NUT?

Kate read the words a second time. A flutter of excitement moved up her spine. "Miss Markham, could you please come in here?" she called. "I want you to see this. It's weird."

"I am ready to leave, Kate. I am standing by the door with my coat on. My hand is on the doorknob."

"Has this computer been acting funny lately?"

"I am opening the door, Kate."

"Wait! It's happening again!"

> REPEAT. I HAVE A MESSAGE FOR THE COM-
> PUTER NUT. WILL YOU RECEIVE? INPUT YES OR
> NO.

"I am stepping outside, Kate."

"Miss Markham, somebody is sending me a message. I cannot believe this. On the computer! Somebody saw my portrait and they're sending me a message."

"I am closing the door, Kate."

"Wait! Let me get my message! I— Oh, all right! I'm coming!"

Hurriedly Kate put her hands on the keybqard and typed one word:

> TOMORROW.

Then she got to her feet and turned off the computer. The screen dimmed and, holding her self-portrait in one hand, she ran for the door.

The Missing Message

"The craziest thing happened to me this afternoon," Kate said. She came into the living room and plopped down on the sofa by her father.

"Tell it quickly, Kate," her mother said, "because your dad's going to be on TV after this commercial. He's promoting National Health Week."

"Go ahead, hon," her father said. "What happened?"

"Well, I was at the office using the computer—this was for school. I was *not* wasting time. I was doing a self-portrait for art. So, anyway, after I finished the picture of myself—it was entitled 'Self-Portrait of a Computer

Nut'—a message came on the computer for me. Someone contacted me!"

"A message? Who was it from?"

"I don't know, Mom. It was practically science fiction. The message just—"

"Shhh, here I am," her father said.

"Kate, I do not like strangers contacting—"

"Later, Mom." Kate turned to watch her father on television. He shifted on the soft sofa cushion. She was suddenly uneasy. What had happened to her that afternoon had been exciting, and now it had suddenly been changed into something for her mother to worry about.

She glanced sideways at her parents. They were leaning forward, as intent on the TV screen as Kate had been earlier on the video screen. Suddenly her father slumped. "Am I that fat?" he asked.

"No, Sam. You know the camera makes everybody appear a little heavier."

"A little heavier than who? Jackie Gleason?"

"Hush, Sam, we want to hear what you're saying."

"I'll tell you what I'm saying! I'm telling people to lose weight and have regular checkups. *I* am telling *them* to lose weight!"

"Sam!"

Kate waited with her self-portrait in her lap. As soon as her father's interview was over, she would slip out. Then maybe her mother would forget the message and . . .

"Thank you, Dr. Morrison," the announcer said, "and

we'll be right back with sports after this message from Bunny Bread."

Kate got up.

"That was very informative, Sam," Kate's mother said. Then she turned to her daughter. "Now, Kate, sit back down and we'll talk about this computer message."

Kate sighed. "It was nothing, Mom, really."

"You have no idea who the message was from?" Kate shook her head. "Honestly, these computers are getting as bad as telephones. I don't like it. Anybody can contact you."

"Mom, you don't understand. *Anybody* cannot—"

"Let me finish. I do not want you to give out your name and address over the computer. I mean it. Any weirdo can—"

"I cannot believe this," Kate said. "For once in my life something interesting has happened, and all you can do is talk about the dangers. If I came home and said I'd been elected President of the United States, you'd say, 'Well, I do not want you going to foreign countries because blah . . . blah . . . blah.' "

"Kate, we care about you. We—Kate, don't turn away. Sam, talk to your daughter."

Dr. Morrison straightened. He said, "Well, I would like to see the self-portrait my beautiful daughter did on the computer." He smiled and held out his hand.

Kate looked down at the sheet of paper in her hand. Without smiling back, she handed it to him.

Her father held the picture up to the light. "And after somebody saw this, they sent you a message?"

"Yes, why? Do you think it's funny-looking?" Kate leaned over his arm and took another look.

"It's not funny-looking at all, Kate," her mother said. "It's very nicely done, but getting back to—"

Abruptly Kate pulled the sheet of paper from her father. "You never like anything I do."

"Kate!"

"It's true. That is the story of my artistic life—total rejection."

"Kate, that's not fair. We like your—"

"You know what this reminds me of?" Kate stepped away from her parents, toward the door. "In kindergarten one time I drew a picture of the world—the entire world! How many people do you know who have drawn a picture of the entire world? I remember Miss Elliot gave me a special sheet of newsprint, and I drew and drew, and when I got through there was this enormous green ball with trees and mountains and foreign people popping out all over it, and I was so proud, and I brought it home and you would not let me hang it on the refrigerator. You said it was too big! You said it covered the ice-water dispenser!"

"Kate!"

"And now, seven years later, I overcome my trauma and bring home another picture and it's the same thing.

I just hope my art teacher is going to be more impressed than you are."

"Kate, we love your picture, don't we, Sam?"

"I'm sorry I bothered you."

Kate stormed into the hall. As she heard her parents begin talking behind her, their voices low with concern, she slowed down to listen. She sighed with relief. She had stopped the lecture on computer communication before her mother made her promise not to answer any more messages.

Kate heard her sister laughing, and she paused in the doorway to Cassie's bedroom.

Cassie was bent over her princess phone, listening. She laughed again. Kate leaned against the door, waiting for her sister to look up.

Cassie said, "Me too! I thought the field goal was good! Everybody around me did! Everybody was yelling and hugging everybody, so I turned and hugged this boy beside me. I thought we had won the game!" More laughter. "Yes, and then come to find out the field goal wasn't good! And I go, 'Well, I do not believe this. I've hugged you, and I don't even know your name, and we've lost the game!' "

In the doorway Kate said, "Cassie."

Cassie held up her hand. She was listening to her phone conversation again. She laughed. Then she put one hand over the receiver and asked Kate, "Is supper ready?"

"No. I finished my self-portrait." She held it up.

"Great. You'll have to do one of me."

"And afterward," Kate went on, "I got this message and—"

Cassie lifted her hand to stop Kate. Into the phone she said, "That's him! That's who it was! And then, when we were leaving the stadium he . . ."

Kate walked down the hall and into her bedroom. Harvey, the family dog, was lying on her bed. Harvey shifted uneasily, knowing that he was not allowed on the furniture. He waited, ears back, for the command to get down.

"Harvey, want to see my self-portrait?"

The tone of Kate's voice started his tail wagging. He was safe.

"There it is."

Harvey sniffed at the sheet of paper and lowered his head to his paws. He closed his eyes.

"And, Harvey, somebody sent me a message!"

Harvey's short tail thumped against the bedspread. He never could resist enthusiasm.

"That's the way I feel too," Kate said. "And, Harvey, I'm going to find out who it is!"

The Chocolate Milk Test

"Wait a minute! This is exactly like something I saw on television."

It was noon, and Kate and her friend Linda were walking into the school cafeteria. "See," Linda went on, pausing to get a tray, "this boy and girl started communicating by computer, and they met in McDonald's and fell in love. That's about all I got to see. My sister claimed she had to watch *General Hospital* for extra credit in Science, and my mom believed her. My mom believes everything my sister says. My sister goes, 'My geography teacher wants us to watch *Dallas*,' and my mom'll go, 'Linda, turn off *Nova* this minute. Your sister's got to watch *Dallas*.'"

"Linda, this is nothing like that program. I don't know who sent this message. It could have been a girl or a boy or a ninety-year-old man. You don't understand—"

"Of course I don't understand. How could I? I have never in my life touched a computer that it didn't go, 'Illegal Command.' Even games. 'Bad input.' I finally agreed—this was over at Roz Hammond's—to play Yatze on her Apple because I used to like it when we had the little pads of paper and the dice and—"

"Linda, will you hush for a minute and listen?"

"Listening is not what I do best."

"Well, try. This was *not* a game. This was somebody trying to contact me, somebody I don't even know, and all my mom could say was, 'Don't give out your name. It's some weirdo.' "

"What did your dad say?"

"My dad did not say anything. My dad was depressed because he looked fat on television."

"Your dad looks fat off television too. Don't tell him I said that."

"I won't."

"You know what my dad's depressed about?"

"Your grades?"

"No, that's what he ought to be depressed about. He's depressed because he thinks his chin is disappearing." She laughed.

"There's nothing wrong with your dad's chin."

"He thinks there is. So, listen, this was so funny. His

picture was in the newspaper last week, and me and my sisters saw it first, and we took an eraser and gently erased his chin—you couldn't tell we'd touched it—and then we folded the newspaper back up and put it in the driveway, and when my dad opened it and saw himself without a chin—well, we had to go in the kitchen, we laughed so hard."

Kate said, "I'll have pizza," to the cafeteria worker and turned back to Linda. "Come with me to my dad's office this afternoon and we'll see if the message comes through again."

"I can't."

"Please, Linda."

"I *can't*. My mom's got me a tutor. My mom managed to find the ugliest math tutor in the entire university. He looks like—who is that man on M*A*S*H who dresses in women's clothes?"

"Klinger."

"He looks like Klinger. H—" Suddenly Linda stopped. The plate containing her hamburger rattled on her tray. She said, "I know who contacted you."

"What?"

"On the computer yesterday. I know who it was."

"Who?"

"Are you ready for this? Frank Wilkins."

"Oh, Linda."

"It has to be. He's always fooling with computers. All he talks about is his software and floppy disks. He's as bad a nut as you are. And don't forget that time he sat by you on the bus and told you he loved you."

"Linda, he was being initiated into a club, and he had to sit by the first girl he came to, and I just happened to be—"

"I know it's him. I have an instinct about these things. I tell you what we'll do. Let's walk out of the cafeteria the same time he does—see, he's sitting right over there with Bubba Joe Riley. Bubba Joe is so disgusting. He's licking pizza sauce off his wrist. Anyway, we will just very casually, very naturally bump into him, and when he looks at you and you look at him we'll know. Come on. Eat fast."

"Linda," Kate said. She pulled out her chair and sat. "You do not understand computers. You can't communicate with just anybody. There are lines connecting computers. You—"

"Listen, if people can rob banks by computer and steal atomic secrets by computer—which I learned on *In the News* Saturday morning during the Bugs Bunny show—well, then Frank Wilkins can send you a message."

Kate looked down at her pizza. "Linda, this is stupid. I would be the last person Frank Wilkins would contact. Ever since he had to tell me he loved me, he's hated me."

"Oh, he's getting up. They're through. Come on. We can eat outside. Hurry or we'll miss our chance."

"Linda, this is stupid."

"Come on. I'll make it look natural. Leave everything to me."

Linda tore across the cafeteria, pulling Kate behind her like a toy. They dodged people, chairs, tables until they were directly behind Frank Wilkins and Bubba Joe Riley. Then they slowed to a walk.

"Just act natural," Linda said.

Bubba Joe was licking pizza sauce off his shirt cuff now. Frank was saying, "Moss claims I was in on it, but I went straight home after school. I worked on my program. My mom will swear I—"

Linda took Kate by the arm. Kate felt as helpless as if she were in a game of Crack the Whip.

With her eyes on Frank's back, Linda closed the remaining distance, waiting for the right moment. "Get ready," she said. Frank lifted his milk carton to drink. "Go!"

And Linda pushed Kate forward at the exact moment when Frank stopped by the trash can to finish his chocolate milk.

She hit Frank Wilkins full force. He swirled around, and she stumbled backwards. He was scowling. He had chocolate milk dripping down his blue sweater. He wiped his chin. He said, "What's wrong with you?"

Kate kept backing into the cafeteria. She flicked her hair behind her ears. Her face burned.

"Why don't you look where you're going?" He glared from Kate to his sweater, then in distaste at his wet hand.

"She stumbled," Linda said. "She just, you know, stumbled. She's sorry."

"Yeah, she's sorry all right."

Frank slam-dunked his milk carton into the trash can and walked into the hall. Still wiping his sweater, he said, "I sat by that stupid girl one time on the school bus, and she's been after me ever since."

Kate and Linda watched in silence as the boys disappeared down the hall.

"Oh, Linda, that was horrible!" Kate said.

"Well, how did I know he was going to stop so suddenly?"

"Did you hear what he said? He thinks I'm after him!"

"He thinks everybody's after him. Anyway, we have narrowed the possibilities. I think we can safely say it is not Frank Wilkins who is contacting you." Linda leaned against the doorway. She began to laugh. "Did you see the expression on his face? It was so funny!"

"He was furious!"

"Frank Wilkins cannot stand to have a hair out of place. He thinks he's Mr. Perfect. Did you see your pizza stuck on his back?"

Kate looked down in horror at the paper napkin in her hand. Her slice of pizza was gone.

"I wish I could be there when he finds out he has been walking around school with a piece of pizza on his back. He has noooo sense of humor. In English we will be sitting there laughing at something, and he'll be going, 'What's everybody laughing at? What's so funny?' And Ervin Bubeck will tell him, and he'll go, 'Oh,' and start combing his hair."

"I just feel terrible, Linda."

"I don't. It made my day. Anyway, do not worry. We will find the answer to who is contacting you on the computer. I promise you that. I am making it my own personal project."

To Kate, it sounded somehow like a threat. She threw her napkin in the trash can and, head lowered, followed Linda down the hall.

The Star Ship

It was Saturday morning, and rain had been coming down for three hours, a cold, solid October rain that brought winter closer.

Kate came into her father's office, shaking rain from her slicker. She threw back her hood and crossed to the door to the computer room. "It is pouring," she said to Miss Markham.

"I'm surprised your mother let you out on a day like this."

"She almost didn't. She said, 'Just because your father is a doctor is no reason to take chances with your health . . . blah . . . blah . . . blah.' And I said, 'I never take chances with my health because when I get sick I have to take free samples.' "

"Kate!"

"That's what my mother said. 'Kate!' Anyway, it's true. I have never had drugstore medicine in my life. How much longer are you going to be?"

"Until I finish the bills."

"But that'll be hours!"

"Well, I'm going to take a break in five minutes. How about that?"

"That's better."

Kate walked to the window. She looked out at the rain-swept street. She closed the blinds, opened them to the same scene, closed them.

"What is wrong with you?" Miss Markham asked without looking around. "Why are you so restless?"

"I'm not restless. I just want to know who sent me that message. And I would like to find out before Linda completely ruins me. Yesterday she—" Kate broke off.

"She what?"

"Nothing."

Kate opened the blinds again. The memory of being pushed into Frank Wilkins, of leaving a slice of pizza on his back, had been returning like an echo to embarrass her again and again. Even now her cheeks reddened. She turned from the window with a sigh.

"Okay, okay, the computer is yours. I need to make some phone calls anyway. Mrs. Brown thinks Arthur swallowed some of the dog's worm pills." She slipped out the accounting program. "I'll be back in twenty minutes, Kate."

Kate slid into the chair as Miss Markham got up. She took a deep breath and exhaled. Before Miss Markham was out of the room, she had begun to type.

THIS IS THE COMPUTER NUT. DOES SOMEBODY
OUT THERE HAVE A MESSAGE FOR ME?

She waited, watching the screen. She moistened her dry lips. She typed again.

REPEAT. THIS IS THE COMPUTER NUT. IS THERE
A MESSAGE FOR ME?

She waited. When nothing happened, she gave a mock scream of impatience.

"Give it a chance," Miss Markham called from her desk.

"I *hate* to wait for anything. You know that." Kate turned back to the video screen. She drummed her fingers on the desk. "I just *hate* to—"

Suddenly Kate straightened. Words were appearing on the screen.

COMPUTER NUT, THAT IS AFFIRMATIVE. THIS
IS BB-9 AND I WAS TRYING TO CONTACT YOU.

"BB-9?" Kate asked herself. "I wonder what that stands for—some sort of program?"

She typed:

> I AM UNFAMILIAR WITH BB-9. WHAT DOES
> THAT STAND FOR?

The answer came at once:

> BB-9 IS A SHORTENED VERSION OF MY DESIG-
> NATION. MY FULL DESIGNATION IS BB-947-82-A-
> 1070-BLX-09. THAT IS A CODE THAT WOULD
> HAVE NO MEANING TO YOU AT THIS TIME. LET
> ME SAY THAT YOU ARE IN CONTACT WITH A
> PEACEABLE BEING WITHOUT MALICE OF IN-
> TENT WHOSE INTEREST IS IN MUTUAL EX-
> CHANGE OF INFORMATION.

Kate paused. Suddenly she wished Linda were there with her to laugh, to wonder at the real identity of BB-9, to yell, "I know who it is, Kate!" She swallowed and typed:

> HOW DID YOU HAPPEN TO SEE MY SELF-
> PORTRAIT?

She waited.

> I SAW IT ON MY MASTER CONSOLE WHICH
> MONITORS ALL TERRESTRIAL TERMINALS.
> YOUR SELF-PORTRAIT WAS THE ONLY INTER-
> ESTING THING ON THE MASTER CONSOLE AT
> 16:39 THURSDAY. ALSO YOU LOOKED AS IF
> YOU HAD A SENSE OF HUMOR, AS IF YOU

WOULD ENJOY A GOOD LAUGH. THAT IS WHY I
DECIDED TO CONTACT YOU.

Kate stared at the words. "Somebody is putting me on."

"Oh, is your message coming?" Miss Markham called
from the outer office.

"*Something's* coming."

"Well, tell me about it when you get through."

Kate let out her breath between her teeth, then typed:

WHERE, EXACTLY, IS THIS MASTER CONSOLE?
HOW FAR AWAY?

She put one hand under her chin and watched the screen.
"Well?"

THE MASTER CONSOLE IS 2591.82 MILES DI-
RECTLY ABOVE YOU AT THIS MOMENT, MOV-
ING IN A GEOSYNCHRONOUS ORBIT.

"Oh, come on. You expect me to believe that?" Kate
put her hands on the keyboard.

WHAT ARE YOU? A SATELLITE? A—

"I'm ready to use the computer now, Kate," Miss Markham called.

"I'm almost through."

The answer was coming. Kate leaned forward.

NO SATELLITE, COMPUTER NUT. I AM IN A
SELF-CONTAINED UNIT, A STAR SHIP, AS YOU

EARTHLINGS WOULD SAY, AND I HAVE BEEN
MONITORING EARTH'S COMPUTERS IN PREPA-
RATION FOR AN OCTOBER LANDING.

Kate snorted with disgust. "An October landing. Who does he think he is? E.T.?"

AND JUST HOW, WHEN, AND WHERE ARE YOU
GOING TO MAKE THIS LANDING?

She waited, leaning forward on her elbows.

THE ACTUAL DETAILS OF MY LANDING CAN-
NOT BE REVEALED AT THIS TIME. HOWEVER, I
WOULD BE GLAD TO DEPICT MY SPACE TRANS-
PORT. IT IS NOT AN UNUSUAL VEHICLE—MUCH
LIKE OTHERS THAT HAVE COME TO YOUR
PLANET—BUT IF IT WOULD BE OF INTEREST TO
YOU . . .

Kate typed:

IT WOULD DEFINITELY BE OF INTEREST.

"Kate, are you finished?" Miss Markham called.
"Just let me see this spaceship," Kate called back.
"Spaceship?"
"Yes, some nut is pretending to be from outer space, and he is going to draw his spaceship. It's nothing out of the ordinary, just some little vehicle he's been tooling around the galaxy in."

"This I gotta see."

Miss Markham came into the room and stood behind Kate. They watched the screen as lines began to appear. For a moment there was not a sound in the office.

Then, when the picture was finished, Miss Markham let out her breath in a low whistle. "Well," she said, "as space vehicles go, that is not bad."

Kate slapped her hands down on the desk. "I hate it when people try to put me on. I *hate* it."

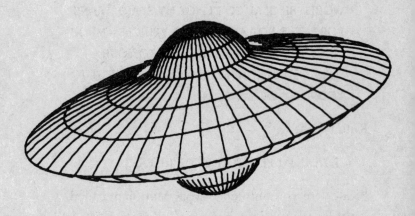

"Don't be so intense, hon. You take life too seriously. It's just somebody playing a joke on you. Go along with it. Ask him to send a picture of himself, of his planet."

Kate kept staring at the spaceship until the picture disappeared and words replaced it on the screen.

WHAT DID YOU THINK OF MY SPACESHIP,
COMPUTER NUT? WAS IT A DISAPPOINTMENT?
WAS IT AS YOU EXPECTED?

"Tell him, 'Yes.' Tell him you'd like to go for a ride. Tell him you'll meet him out in front of the office. Ask him if he's got an alien friend for me." Miss Markham broke off and let her hands drop onto Kate's shoulders. "I am getting carried away. Whatever you tell him will have to be some other time. I need the computer now."

Kate typed:

COMPUTER NUT LOGGING.

"There." Kate got up and walked to the window. She stared out at the wet street.

"You'll find out who it is," Miss Markham said.

Kate flicked her hair behind her ears. "I'm beginning to wonder," she said.

A New Suspect

"I have had the most humongously horrible morning of my life," Linda said.

"Me too," Kate answered. "I just got back from my dad's office, and remember that person who—"

"Wait. Let me tell mine first," Linda said. "Mine's the worst."

"Oh, all right."

Kate settled herself on the sofa and stretched out her legs. In her years of friendship with Linda, Kate had gotten used to going second. She propped the phone against a pillow and prepared for a long story.

"Well, this was the day for my math tutor. Remember I told you about him? So he comes and we sit at the kitchen table, which is the absolute center of the universe! Everybody comes through and makes fun of me—my sisters, their friends. My mom is pretending to cook. My dad is pretending to fix the disposal. And in the middle of all this, I am supposed to be learning long division. Big numbers—14,988 divided by 4521! Which is ridiculous! When am I ever going to have that many of anything?"

Linda drew in a deep breath. "Anyway, I could not get one right—some of them didn't even come out even. And my mom started yelling, 'You're not trying . . . blah . . . blah . . . blah.' She's like *Mommie Dearest* when she gets mad, and Dad started yelling, 'What do you expect? She's *your* daughter.' And the tutor yelled, 'She got one! She got one!' And while I was sitting there wondering which one I got, he gave me twenty-five problems as homework and left. I am really depressed."

"You ought to get a computer."

"Can your dad's computer do long division?"

"Linda, I have a Mickey Mouse computer from first grade that can do long division."

"Can I borrow it?"

"Sure."

"That makes me feel better. If it were cute—the tutor—I wouldn't mind so much. I learn better when I have a cute teacher. Well, it's your turn. What terrible thing happened to you?"

"Oh." Kate sat up. "Remember I told you about the computer message?"

"Vaguely."

"Well, this morning I walked through the pouring rain, seven blocks, and it turned out to be some kook pretending to be from outer space. He drew a picture of his spaceship and talked about his orbit and—"

Linda took a deep breath. "Kate, I know who it is!"

"Linda, don't start that again."

"The minute you said 'kook,' it came to me."

"Linda—"

"You are going to hate this, Kate, because it is somebody we both scorn, but the minute you said 'kook,' you know who I thought of?"

"Who?"

"Willie Lomax."

"Willie Lomax! Don't be ridiculous."

"It *has* to be him. He loves practical jokes—remember that time in home room with the fish bowl and the toilet paper? Remember that anonymous call to the principal about the stink bomb? And he's great with computers. He was at computer camp with you—you told me so. It is definitely Willie."

Kate dangled her legs off the sofa. She dropped her shoes to the floor and eyed her feet critically. Her socks had gotten wet during the walk to her dad's office, and her shoes had dyed them brown.

"Mmmmmm," she said, pretending not to be interested. She did not want Linda to suspect that she liked Willie Lomax a lot. After computer camp she had told Linda that Willie was funny, and Linda had said, "Don't tell me you *like* Willie Lomax!" "No, I just think he's funny," Kate had said quickly, and Linda had answered, "I was afraid you had lost your smarts."

"It *is* him," Linda went on enthusiastically. "And I know how we can prove it."

"No!" Kate got to her feet. "Absolutely no!"

The thought of Willie Lomax saying something like, "That stupid girl's been after me ever since computer camp," made her face burn.

"You are not pushing me into Willie Lomax! I mean it, Linda. Yesterday Frank Wilkins came up to me and told me that if the pizza sauce didn't come out of his sweater, I was going to have to pay for it."

"He told me the same thing. I think I dislike him intensely. Anyway, here's what I have in mind."

"I don't want to hear it."

"Yes, you do. It's perfect. Willie Lomax is in Honor Society, and tomorrow afternoon they are having a dog wash to make money. So we take our dogs over to be washed. What could be more natural than that?"

"It would be a lot more natural, Linda, if you had a dog."

"So we take your dog. Three dollars a dog—you have to admit that's a bargain. All we have to do is make sure that Willie is the one who washes Harvey. Then, while the washing is in progress, you casually make some comment about computers and watch his reaction. The plan is foolproof. You find out if it's Willie and get a clean dog at the same time. If you want him dipped in flea dip, it's a dollar more."

"I don't know, Linda," Kate said slowly. She sat back down.

"Don't you want to find out who it is?"

"Yes."

She admitted to herself that she also wanted to see Willie Lomax washing dogs. Still she hesitated. With Linda along, the possibility of something going wrong was great.

"Don't you want to eliminate Willie Lomax as a possibility?"

"Yes, of course."

"Then let's go to the dog wash. It'll be something to do. Sunday afternoons are so boring anyway."

"I just don't think it's Willie, Linda. He's got an Apple computer, and there is no way he could connect it to my dad's."

"You just don't want to think it's Willie. You want to think it's somebody new and good-looking."

"Not really."

"Come on. Let's go."

Kate smiled at the thought of Willie Lomax washing a dog. She said, "Oh, all right."

"Great! I'll be over tomorrow afternoon. Look at it this way—what can go wrong?"

The Trouble
with Flea Dip

Linda and Kate were making their way toward the parking lot of the school. It was Sunday afternoon, three o'clock, and the dog wash had been in progress for an hour.

"Not so fast," Linda said. "I don't want to get there until we spot Willie Lomax."

Kate had already spotted him in the last line with his sleeves rolled up, his hair falling over his forehead. "I don't want to get there at all," she said. She tugged Harvey's leash. "Calm down, Harvey."

Harvey had been straining his leash ever since they had rounded the corner and he had caught sight of the group in the school parking lot—dogs, dozens of them. He pulled

forward, choked on his collar and, unconcerned, pulled
forward again. He thought he saw and smelled several old
enemies in the ragged lines.

"Sit, Harvey," Kate said.

Harvey was beyond obeying. Behind his bangs, his black
eyes were bright, beady, intent. He threw himself forward.

"Hold him back," Linda said. "Honestly, I'm sorry we
brought him."

"We could hardly come to a dog wash without him."

"Did you tell me he graduated from obedience school
or dropped out? Oh, look, there's Willie."

"Where?"

"In the last line, and he's only got two dogs waiting—
a Boston terrier and a poodle. They ought to go fast."

Linda and Kate crossed the street, with Harvey, leash
stretched tight, in the lead. They made their way across
the school yard and got in the last line behind the poodle.
The woman glanced at Harvey and quickly picked up her
poodle.

"Muffin's allergic to other dogs," the woman explained.
Harvey lifted his leg in the direction of her shoe.

"Harvey!" Kate pulled him back against her leg and
shortened his leash. She could feel his eager breath hot
against her ankle.

"Willie is not much of a dog washer," Linda commented
behind her hand. "Look at him. He looks like he's knead-
ing dough." She laughed.

Kate let herself look at Willie for the first time. He was

washing a schnauzer. His rolled-up sleeves were damp with water. "Almost through, Nicky," he told the struggling dog. The dog's tongue was hanging out the side of his mouth; his eyes rolled toward his master.

"You want the flea dip?" Willie asked. He wiped soap suds off his cheek with the back of one hand. "It's a dollar more."

"Yes."

"Sorry, pal," Willie told the schnauzer.

Kate glanced down at Harvey. He was sniffing the spot where the poodle had been sitting. Smelling was one of his primary pleasures. Suddenly he caught a different scent. He looked up.

His tail stopped wagging. His beady eyes sharpened. His ears pointed forward. Boomer, his worst enemy in the world, was at the front of the next line, pressed against his owner, his tail curled between his legs.

Harvey twitched with excitement. He barked once. Boomer was too upset to notice. The smell of dog shampoo and flea dip had reduced him to a blob of dread. His long legs trembled like twigs.

Willie Lomax lowered the schnauzer into the garbage can of flea dip, then dried him. He glanced up. "Who's next?"

"Inger's next," the lady with the Boston terrier said.

As Willie reached up to take Inger, he caught sight of Linda and Kate at the back of his line. Quickly he ducked his head.

"Now did you see that?" Linda asked. "As soon as he saw you, he looked down. He could not meet your eyes. That is a sure sign of guilt. Ask any psychologist."

"Maybe," Kate said. She herself had looked away at the same moment.

"It's him, all right."

Willie took the Boston terrier. The boy beside Willie was washing a sheep dog and said, "Hey, Willie, how come you get all the little dogs?"

"This is the express lane, man, nothing over ten pounds." Willie turned the hose on the terrier. Inger's eyes bulged in panic.

"See," Linda said, "he is so flustered that he sprayed that little dog right in the face."

Harvey's eyes had not left Boomer. Boomer was now under the hose himself. He had begun to whimper with fear. Harvey had never heard his enemy make such a sound. He tried to take a few steps forward but could not move on his shortened leash.

Kate said absently, "Sit, Harvey." She had begun to feel it had been a mistake to come. If Willie *was* sending the messages, then she would probably scare him off by . . .

"Now, when we get up there," Linda said, "you make some comment about computers that will let him know you're on to him."

"If I can think of anything."

"*If* you can! I thought you already had!"

The boy next to Willie said, "Come on, Lomax, help

me get this spaniel in the garbage can. You been goofing off all afternoon."

"Wait till I finish Inger. You want the flea dip, ma'am?"

"Inger doesn't have fleas."

"Well, there you are then."

Willie walked over to where his friend was struggling to get Boomer into the garbage can. He hiked up his wet sleeves.

"Grab his legs, Willie."

"Right." Willie took Boomer by the hind legs. "This dog does not want to be dipped. He's holding on with his toes. Did you ever see that Road Runner cartoon where Coyote was . . ."

Harvey twitched with excitement. He had never seen his enemy in such peril. Boomer's ears were flattened against his head. His eyes, wide with fear, rolled from side to side. A steady moan came from his throat. It was obviously the moment to attack.

Harvey lunged forward. He was held tight by the leash, but he twisted suddenly in a move that had brought him success in the past. His head slipped out of his collar, and he dashed toward Boomer and the garbage can.

In three strides he was there. A powerful leap lifted his short legs off the ground, and he aimed straight for the white of Boomer's trembling throat.

"Harvey!" Kate started after him.

Willie and his friend were lowering Boomer into the flea dip. "This is like dipping an octopus," Willie said.

"He's got more legs than any dog I ever—"

"Harvey!"

Then Willie looked up. He was just in time to see Harvey fling himself into the air, to hear the thud against the garbage can, and to feel the warm wave of flea dip slap into his chest. He fell backward with the garbage can and Boomer in his lap. He struggled to get up while Boomer and Harvey waged an awkward dog fight in his lap.

"Harvey! Come!" Kate caught him by the back legs and pulled him, struggling, out of the way. Then she looked down at Willie.

"Oh, I'm so sorry. My dog slipped out of his collar. Let me get this garbage can. Let me—"

"No, you've done enough already." Willie did not glance up. The wave of laughter from the other dog washers hurt more than the jolt of his fall. Trying not to show pain, he got to his feet.

Kate darted forward. "Let me—"

"No!"

The force of the word caused Kate to step back as if she had been slapped. She watched helplessly as Willie shook water from his arms, wrung out his shirttail. Someone took Boomer. "Thank you," he managed to say. Then he looked at Kate.

"If you want to do something, you can take your dog to somebody else's line."

"Look, she said she was sorry," Linda said. "You don't have to be so irritable."

"Yeah, Lomax, at least you got rid of your fleas," a dog washer called.

Linda laughed and then trailed off as Willie turned his cold glance on her.

Kate looked away. Her eyes stung with tears. Spots of color flushed her cheeks. She bent and worked Harvey's collar over his head. "Let's go," she said without looking up.

"We don't have to leave just because Willie Lomax got a little flea dip on—"

"Come!"

Kate spoke so sharply that Harvey thought it was a command. Dutifully he began to trot forward. The event had not turned out exactly as he had hoped. He had gotten his teeth into Boomer, but Boomer had tasted like flea dip. Well, a partial success . . .

With one final glance at the dog wash, Harvey took the lead for home.

The Creature
from the Computer

"Well, at least we have learned one thing. It *was* Willie Lomax," Linda said as they were walking home.

"We haven't learned anything, Linda, except that we made fools of ourselves." Kate was glad to be facing into the wind. The tears in her eyes had dried without spilling over.

"Harvey made fools of us, didn't you, boy?" Linda leaned down and scratched his head. "Bad dog."

Harvey enjoyed praise. He wagged his short tail.

Linda lifted her head and laughed. "Didn't Willie Lomax look hilarious sprawled on the ground, covered with flea dip?"

"Anybody would."

"I bet he smells funny for a week."

Kate did not answer. She watched the red and yellow leaves under her feet without pleasure.

"Oh, listen, I just had a terrific idea."

"No! I don't want to hear it. *No!"*

"Just listen, Kate. This really is perfect, the final proof. We go to your dad's office right now and we—"

"It's Sunday. It's not open," Kate said with obvious relief.

"Well, we can talk your dad into opening it. I know we can once he understands the importance of the situation. So we go over there and you get on the computer and send a message."

"What message?"

"Anything. It doesn't matter. We just want to see if there's an answer. Willie can't answer. Obviously he is on his way home to dry out."

Kate hesitated.

"Look, it's the first idea I've had that can't in any way make us look stupid. And I'm getting interested in this." As they turned the corner Linda added, "There's your dad. He just finished washing the car. Perfect timing. Let me ask him. Remember that time I talked him into driving us to Frodo's for pizza?"

"And then made him wait out in the car."

"I had to. If he'd known he drove me over there to see

Tommy Ryan, he'd— Oh, Dr. Morrison, wait. Don't go in the house. Would you do us a biiiiig favor?"

Kate and Linda sat in front of the computer, sharing the chair. "Go ahead, start," Linda said. She pretended to wring her hands like a mad scientist.

Kate put her hands on the keyboard and typed:

> THIS IS THE COMPUTER NUT. I HAVE A MES-
> SAGE FOR BB-9. ARE YOU THERE? WILL YOU
> RECEIVE?

"Perfect," Linda said.

The two girls waited, leaning forward slightly, watching the screen.

"Do it again."

> REPEAT. THIS IS THE COMPUTER NUT. I WOULD
> LIKE TO CONTACT BB-9. WILL YOU RECEIVE?

"He *would* receive," Linda said, "if he weren't on his way home, dripping flea dip all over the sidewalk." She laughed. "This is fun. I'm beginning to see why you like computers."

Another minute passed.

"How long does it usually take?" Linda asked. "I want some action."

"Well, last time the answer came immediately."

"Let's give it five minutes, and then we'll get your dad to drive us past Willie's house, and we'll—"

Suddenly Linda broke off. Her mouth dropped open in surprise. Words were appearing on the video screen.

THIS IS BB-9. SORRY FOR THE DELAY. I AM
READY TO RECEIVE YOUR MESSAGE NOW. GO
AHEAD, COMPUTER NUT.

Kate sat up a little straighter. "He answered." She glanced at Linda. "So what am I supposed to say? What is my big message?"

Linda shrugged.

"Linda, you made me do this, and now I don't have any message. I feel like a fool." The thought of Willie Lomax possibly waiting for the message, cold, wet, smelling of flea dip, his brown eyes squinting with fury . . .

"Just fake it. Make something up."

"Like what?"

"The message is . . ." Linda paused in thought. "The message is that you want to see a picture of him. Perfect! He's seen you. You want to see him. Go ahead. Type. Type!"

Kate hesitated.

"You *do* want to see a picture of him, don't you?"

"Yes."

"Then type!"

BB-9, WE WOULD LIKE TO SEE A PICTURE OF
YOU.

Kate leaned back in the chair and waited, her fingers resting on the keys.

YOU WROTE 'WE.' YOU ARE NOT ALONE?
SOMEONE IS THERE WITH YOU?

"Don't tell him it's me," Linda said. "Willie Lomax has never liked me since I told on him in third grade for drawing a naked picture of Miss Ellis on the sidewalk."

YES, A FRIEND IS WITH ME. WE WOULD BOTH
LIKE TO SEE WHAT YOU LOOK LIKE. YOU HAVE
SEEN MY SELF-PORTRAIT. I'D LIKE TO SEE
YOURS.

"Perfect."
"Stop saying that. It's not perfect. I feel like an idiot."

I THINK THAT YOU DO NOT REALLY WANT TO
SEE WHAT I LOOK LIKE. I THINK YOU AND
YOUR FRIEND WANT TO LAUGH AT ME.

"How did he know that?"
"Well, if it's Willie, he knows you're with me and that you laugh at everything."

WELL, THAT IS ALL RIGHT WITH ME. I DO NOT
MIND PROVIDING HUMOR. IT WILL BE GOOD
PRACTICE FOR ME.

Kate and Linda sat without moving, watching the screen.

ACTUALLY, I SHOULD HAVE EXPECTED THIS
SORT OF THING. YOUR PLANET IS KNOWN AS
THE LAUGHING PLANET. DID YOU KNOW THAT?
YOURS IS THE ONLY PLANET IN THE WHOLE
UNIVERSE WHERE THERE IS LAUGHING.

"He is weird," Linda said.

I COULD GO ON AND ON. IAXTRON, FOR EX-
AMPLE, IS THE ONLY PLANET WHERE INTELLI-
GENT BEINGS FLY. IT IS KNOWN AS THE
FLYING PLANET. ONE OF THE CHALLENGES OF
VISITING THESE PLANETS IS "CATCHING ON,"
AS YOU SAY, TO WHEN TO LAUGH OR WHEN
TO FLY. FOR EXAMPLE, IT WOULD BE A BIG
MISTAKE ON IAXTRON TO FLY WHILE EATING.
TO DROP A CREAM PIE ON AN IAXTRONIAN,
FOR EXAMPLE, WOULD BE THE GREATEST OF
INSULTS. WHILE TO THROW A CREAM PIE AT
SOMEONE ON EARTH IS ACCEPTABLE, EVEN
HUMOROUS. I TELL YOU THIS SO YOU WILL
KNOW I AM NOT IGNORANT ABOUT HUMOR.

"*Very* weird."

Kate did not answer. She sat, eyes fixed on the screen,
fingers resting on the keyboard.

WOULD YOU LIKE TO SEE MY SELF-PORTRAIT
NOW?

Linda said, "Amen."
Kate typed:

    YES.

And the lines began to appear.

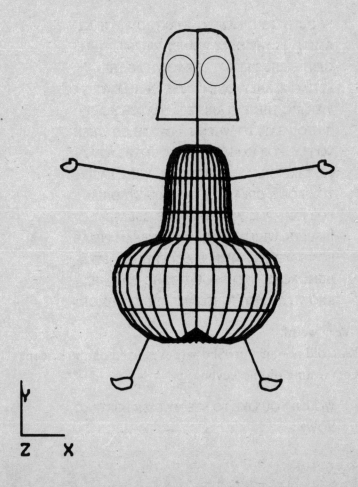

An Unwanted Call

Kate and Linda stared at the screen. When the complete picture had appeared, they sat for a moment without speaking.

Suddenly Linda threw back her head and laughed. "Now I *know* it's Willie Lomax."

"How?"

"The shape's the same!"

"It's not! That's a terrible thing to say. It's—" Kate fell silent. She felt shaken, not by the messages and the picture, not even by the fact that Linda had insulted Willie. It went deeper than that. It was the feeling she had gotten once when she was on the edge of a cliff, enjoying the excitement, and then a certain uneasiness had come, a warning that she could be drawn over.

Almost without thinking, she pushed the button marked "Hard Copy." She took the picture that slid out and stared at it. Her feeling of strangeness grew.

Suddenly Linda straightened. "You know what I'm going to do?" she said excitedly. "I'm going to call the Lomax house and ask to speak to Willie. You keep talking or sending or whatever you call it. Where's the phone book?"

"Linda, don't—"

On the screen words were replacing the picture:

DID YOU RECEIVE MY SELF-PORTRAIT? DID MY
APPEARANCE GIVE YOU AND YOUR FRIEND A
LAUGH?

Linda was flipping through the pages of the phone book. "Aha!" She dialed the number. Kate watched with a worried look and then turned back to the video screen.

She typed:

YOUR PICTURE WAS RECEIVED. YOU LOOKED
EXACTLY THE WAY WE THOUGHT YOU WOULD.

Linda laughed with delight. "That's perfect. Now ask him— Oh, hello, is this the Lomax residence? . . . Is Willie there?" She made a face at Kate. "He is? Could I speak to him, please? . . . Oh, he's busy?" Linda pretended to be Willie typing with one hand on the computer. "No, no message. I'll call back later— Oh, yes, wait, there *is* a message. Tell Willie that Kate Morrison called."

"Linda!"

Kate screeched the word. She jumped up as if she had been stung. Her cheeks burned. She forgot the strange way she had felt a moment before.

"Did you get that? Tell him Kate Morrison called to apologize for Harvey's behavior."

"Linda!" Kate lunged at Linda and tried to grab the phone out of her hand. Linda swirled away, moving the phone out of reach.

"No, that's all, Mrs. Lomax. Bye-bye."

This time Kate grabbed the phone, yanked it out of Linda's hand, and slammed it down. She turned to face Linda, her dark eyes blazing.

"I cannot believe you did that! I cannot believe that somebody I thought was my best friend would do such a terrible thing."

"Kate, I only did it to force Willie out into the open. How else are we going to—"

"Kate," Dr. Morrison called from his outer office, "you and Linda come on. I'm ready to leave."

Kate flipped off the computer without waiting to read the new message that was appearing on the screen.

ACTUALLY, COMPUTER NUT, THAT IS THE LIKE-
NESS OF ONE OF THE ROBOTS ON THE SPACE
VEHICLE. HIS NAME IS ELMER. HE HAS NO
SENSE OF HUMOR BUT I HAVE PROGRAMMED

HIM TO SAY HA-HA WHEN I TELL A JOKE. I
HOPE THE PCTURE OF ELMER MADE YOU
LAUGH. LATER I WILL DRAW MY REAL LIKE-
NESS, OR RATHER THE LIKENESS I WILL AS-
SUME WHEN I—

"I will never forgive you for that," Kate said. She grabbed
her sweater. "I will *never* forgive you. I'm going to call
up Tommy Ryan when I get home and say I'm you."

"Kate!"

"If his mother answers I'm going to say, 'Mrs. Ryan,
please give Tommy a message. Tell him Linda loooooooves
him.' "

"Kate, wait. I didn't do it to be mean. I was just being
funny. I thought you'd laugh."

"Huh!"

"Look, it was just Willie Lomax. I wouldn't have done
it if it was somebody you liked. Kate, wait. Listen!"

In the doorway Kate swirled and faced Linda. "No, *you*
listen. Every time you do something mean to me, you
have the same excuse. It was *funny*. I was just being *funny*."
In her fury she was imitating Linda's voice exactly. "It
was *funny* when you pushed me into Frank Wilkins, and
it was *funny* when you pushed me into the boys' rest room
and held the door and wouldn't let me out, and it was
funny when you—"

She broke off, too angry to remember a third example
of Linda's meanness. "I cannot believe that I have let you

make a fool of me since third grade. I cannot believe it has taken me this long to catch on to what you're doing."

"Girls!" Dr. Morrison called. He was holding the front door open. "Come on. I'm leaving."

Kate continued to glare at Linda. She felt as if she were really looking at her for the first time in years, and she saw nothing in Linda's round, now blank face that would make her want to be Linda's best friend. Indeed, it was suddenly easy to dislike her. "Good-bye." Kate swept out the door, slinging her sweater over her shoulder like Zorro.

Linda remained in the doorway for a moment, stunned by Kate's attack. "I was just trying to be funny," she said to Kate's back. Her chin crumpled with the unfairness of what was happening. She lifted her head. "Kate," she called, "I can't help being funny."

She crossed the waiting room. Tears spilled out of her eyes and rolled down her cheeks. "Kate, you have absolutely no sense of humor."

As she brushed blindly past Dr. Morrison, she said, "Dr. Morrison, tell Kate I didn't do it to be mean. Tell her I was just being funny."

Dr. Morrison locked the office door with a sigh.

The Promise

Cassie came and stood in the doorway of Kate's room.
Kate was lying across the bed, staring up at the ceiling.
The picture of BB-9 was face down on her bedside table.

"The phone's for you," Cassie sang cheerfully from the
doorway. "It's a boyeeeeee."

"Don't be funny." Kate rolled over, put her head on
her arms, and stared down at the carpet. The bones of
her thin, bent back showed through her shirt.

"I'm not kidding. It's a boy and he has a very nice voice.
'May I please speak to Kate.' "

Kate closed her eyes.

"Come on, Kate. He's waiting. It's mean to keep boys waiting on the phone."

"You do it all the time."

"I do not, not since I grew up. I mean, here is some nice boy who has probably spent a half hour working up the nerve to call you. I was over at Marcia's one time, and her brother was calling up Peggy Ballentine, and he sat there going, 'I'll count to ten and then I'll dial . . . nine . . . nine and a half . . . nine and three-quarters,' and so finally he got to ten and dialed and she wouldn't come to the phone. We could hear her whispering, 'Tell him I'm not here,'—Marcia and I were on the upstairs extension, listening, and—"

"Well, I'm not whispering anything. I know exactly who it is."

"Who?"

"Willie Lo-max." Her voice broke on his last name.

"Maybe." Cassie sighed. "All right, so you want me to tell him you're not here?"

"Yes. Tell him—"

Kate stopped. She got to her feet and stormed out of the bedroom. "Never mind. I'll tell him myself." Kate was so upset, her feelings so mixed that there was no single name for the emotion that raced through her body.

She picked up the hall phone. "What do you want, Willie?" she snapped.

"Kate!" Cassie was standing in the doorway, looking

shocked. "I thought you liked Willie Lomax. I—"

Kate turned to glare at her sister while she waited for Willie to answer. "No, I did not call you," she went on in the same hard way. "It was Linda trying to be funny. And, furthermore, if you are the person who is sending me messages on the computer, I wish you would stop!"

Kate slammed down the phone and went back into her bedroom. She flung herself across the bed. The mattress bounced.

"Kate, you were really rude."

"I meant to be."

"And sexist!"

"I am *not* sexist!" Kate turned to look at her sister.

"You are too! If it had been a girl, you wouldn't have snatched up the phone and screamed like a maniac—you'd have given her a chance to say what she wanted. But just let a boy call and you go crazy. You scream and slam down the phone. That's what sexism is—treating people differently because of their sex. You have to learn to think of boys as people."

"I'm *not* being sexist. If Linda called, I would scream and slam down the phone in exactly the same way."

Cassie watched Kate for a moment and then came into the room. She sat on the edge of the bed. "All right, what's wrong?"

"Nothing." Kate kicked off her shoes and let them drop to the floor, one by one. "Everything."

It was moments like this when Kate wanted to be an adult, walking around on a steady world instead of this up-and-down trampoline.

"Like what?" Cassie asked.

"I don't know. It seems like everything's been going wrong since I started getting those messages."

"From the computer?"

"They aren't from the computer, Cassie. They're from *somebody*."

"Or some thing," Cassie said in a low science fiction voice.

"I've had enough humor for one day, thank you."

"I can't help it. Ever since I saw *E.T.* I've had a horror of something being in my closet. Imagine standing there trying to decide what you're going to wear, and long skinny fingers creep out of your dresses. Rrrrrrr." She shuddered. "I'm sorry. Go on with what you were saying."

Kate sat up in bed, cross-legged. "All right. When I first started getting the messages, I was really excited. I thought it was somebody who would turn out to be a friend."

"And it didn't?"

"It didn't turn out to be anybody. So Linda got into the act—you know how she is. She pushed me into Frank Wilkins to see if it was him, and then Willie Lomax got dunked in flea dip because she thought it was him, and I feel awful!"

"I don't imagine Willie Lomax feels too good either."

"And I really liked him, Cassie, and now I feel like I never want to see him again."

"Well, obviously he doesn't feel the same way. He called."

Kate did not answer.

"And if he's the one sending the messages—"

"He's not."

"You're sure of that?"

Kate nodded.

"All right then, as I see it, you have gotten your hopes up about these computer messages, right?"

"I guess."

"And you have allowed yourself to think it's somebody out of this world, right?"

Kate nodded more quickly this time.

"All right, now, be really honest. Can you think of one single person that you know—Frank Wilkins, Willie Lomax—anybody who wouldn't be a disappointment?"

"Well, I don't know . . . I thought maybe it would turn out to be somebody new, somebody I didn't know."

"The people you don't know turn out to be exactly like the people you do know, same faults, same everything. You want some advice?"

"No."

"Here it is anyway. First, apologize to Willie Lomax. Flea dip is really repulsive. Even dogs can't stand it. Then call Linda and smooth that over, and then—"

"Then what?"

"Then forget about those stupid messages."

Kate did not answer. She felt again that pull that comes on the edge of something, something that now was both scary and attractive.

Cassie said, "Give me your solemn promise that you won't send any messages for at least a week."

Kate glanced at her bedside table, where the picture of BB-9 lay, face down. She knew Cassie was right. She, Kate, was being foolish. She was letting herself believe something impossible, the way years ago she had let herself believe in Santa Claus.

"Repeat after me," Cassie said. "I will not send any messages for a week."

Kate sighed. "I will not send any messages for a week."

"And if I do—"

"And if I do—"

"May my lips—"

"May my lips—"

"Turn to dust."

Kate threw a pillow at her sister.

Cassie said, "Believe it or not, that is the actual promise the Theta Alpha Betas have to make—that's a stupid sorority in my school. These girls actually stand there and say, 'May my lips turn to dust if ever I reveal the secrets I have learned here today,' and then they run out and *tell*. One girl even . . ."

And Kate, smiling a little, leaned back to hear the story.

The Apple Decision

"**W**ait! I want to ask you something."

It was Willie Lomax, and he was slightly out of breath from running after Kate. Kate did not break her fast, get-home stride. She had known Willie was behind her. She had heard him call her name at the corner, heard his footsteps. She never wanted to see Willie Lomax again.

That morning, right before English, Kate had managed to apologize to Willie. "I'm sorry about the flea dip and the phone call," she had muttered on her way to the pencil sharpener. She was not even sure he had heard her, but it had upset her enough to make her sharpen her pencil down to a nub. Then she actually had to take an English

test with a pencil an inch and a half long.

"What did you mean about somebody sending you messages on the computer?" Willie asked as he fell into step with her. Kate could no longer pretend he wasn't there. Without glancing at him, she said, "Oh, it's you. Hi."

"Yesterday on the phone, remember you said that if I was the person sending you computer messages, you wanted me to stop?"

Kate looked at him out of the corners of her eyes. "*Are* you the person sending me messages?"

"No."

"Then it doesn't matter."

"But I'm interested."

"Oh, all right. Somebody who is pretending to be from outer space—he calls himself BB-9—has been contacting me on my father's office computer. I know it's somebody playing a joke, and I—well, it was Linda, really—thought it might be you."

He shook his head. Kate thought she smelled the faint odor of flea dip. Probably when he was ninety, in church, someone behind him would say, "Mom, that old man smells like flea dip." She ducked to hide her smile.

"What are you smiling about?"

"Nothing."

"Something about me?"

"No," she lied, "just something about the computer messages."

"When I see people looking amused, I'm always

afraid my pants have split or something."

Kate's smile softened, as if things had suddenly eased between them.

"That actually happened to me one time in a Little League game. I had just made a home run—it was my moment of greatest triumph—it was the winning home run actually, and the whole team came running out and piled on me. It was wonderful. I bent forward under their weight and heard *riiiiip*. It was no longer quite so wonderful. Everyone there laughed."

"BB-9 says we're known as the laughing planet."

"Earth is known as the laughing planet?"

"So BB-9 says."

"Living here never seemed all that hilarious to me. I mean, you sit around waiting for something terrible to happen to somebody—like they fall down in the hall, or their pants split, or they get a spot on their clothes in the wrong place, and you laugh."

Suddenly Willie stopped. "I'd like to see one of these messages. Are you going to your dad's office now?"

"No, I promised my sister I wouldn't. See, it's like my life's been miserable since the messages started so"—she held up her hand—"no more."

Willie tucked his thumbs in his jeans pockets. His dark eyes were thoughtful. "What exactly did you promise your sister?"

"That I would not contact BB-9 for a week."

"Then there's no problem. I'll contact him. That way

you won't be breaking your promise." He waited for the words to sink in.

"No, that wouldn't be right. I really did promise."

"We'll go to my house. *I'll* contact him on *my* Apple. That wouldn't be breaking any promise. Come on."

Kate hesitated. She was tempted. The week ahead looked uninteresting without messages from BB-9. She already missed the reckless excited feeling that came over her with each communication.

Willie sensed she was weakening. "Look at it this way. If BB-9 really is from outer space, which I am frankly very suspicious about—I mean, I have a hard time accepting anything arriving from outer space other than an occasional meteorite or piece of burnt-out space equipment. But if he really is from outer space, then you should be able to contact him on any computer. This would be a good test."

Kate and Willie had stopped walking. They were now standing at the corner of Elm Street, Willie's street. His split-level house was in sight.

"BB-9 did say he monitors everything," Kate went on thoughtfully. "He did say he has a master console that has access to all Earth's computers."

"Which means he would be able to monitor my Apple."

"I guess so."

"Then let's try it."

Kate did not answer. She stood there, her schoolbooks slung to her hip. For a long moment she talked herself out of going to Willie's house. She told herself that no matter how she got around it, she would be breaking a promise to her sister. She told herself she had been better off, happier, before BB-9. She told herself that if she had a grain of sense in her head she would keep on walking down Bryan Street, go straight home, and do her homework.

"Well?" Willie said.

She looked up at him. She grinned. "Let's try it," she said.

A Friend of the Computer Nut

Willie and Kate were in the Lomax family room sitting in front of Willie's Apple. Willie was shouting, "Mom, will you get the brats out of here?" The brats were Willie's little sisters.

"I never thought of you as having all these sisters," Kate said.

"Believe me, it was not my idea. I was seven years old, an only child, very happy. I was even slim back then, and then my mom told me Victoria was going to be born. This is Victoria. Say, 'Hi.' "

"Hi."

"Brilliant child. I thought, well, I can handle that, one

little sister, no problem. It might even be nice to have someone look up to me, adore me. Then Jessica came along. Can you say, 'Hi'?"

Without taking her thumb from her mouth, Jessica said, "Hi," around it.

"And here's Penelope. She's the mean one. Say, 'Hi,' Penelope."

"No!"

"Tell Kate how old you are."

"No!"

"Well, you don't have to hit me." He pinned Penelope's arms to her sides. "Mom, call Penelope! See, she's allowed to hit me, but I'm not allowed to hit back. That's why I have so many bruises. Mom! Kate and I are trying to do our homework!" Then he looked down at his struggling sister. "Penelope, you know something? You make Attila the Hun look sweet."

"No!"

"That's the only word she knows, isn't it, Penelope?"

"No!"

"Girls," Mrs. Lomax called tiredly from the kitchen.

"Mom's calling you. I bet she's got something for you. Go see. Hurry."

As the girls ran from the room, Willie lay back in his chair. "I'm not ever going to have any children." He remained, eyes shut for a moment, resting.

"I think your sisters are cute." She liked Willie even better after seeing him with his sisters.

"They're as cute as baby cobras. That's why I'm in so many school activities—Honor Society, Russian Club, 4-H, Basketball Manager. I'll do anything to keep from baby-sitting. I would be in a Future Farmers of America meeting right now learning about sick chickens if I hadn't wanted to see you."

Willie pulled himself forward. "Now, how do you go about contacting this BB-9?" His brown eyes were suddenly sharp, his expression so intent that Kate knew what he was going to look like when he was a man.

"Well, I just type, 'This is the Computer Nut'—that's what he calls me—'I have a message for BB-9. Will you receive?' "

"And he answers?"

"He always has."

"I better say, 'This is a *friend* of the Computer Nut,' to keep things honest."

"And what if he answers?"

"He's not going to. It's not possible. I'm not hooked up to any other computers. If he does answer—which is impossible unless he really is from outer space—if he does, then I'll ask him to describe himself, something like that."

"I've already got his description." Kate opened her notebook and pulled out the picture of BB-9. Without a word she handed the sheet of paper to Willie.

"This is him?"

"Yes."

"He sent you this?"

"Yes."

Willie regarded the picture of BB-9 for a moment in silence. Then he said, "He does look a little bit like me."

"That's what Linda said."

"Thanks a lot. She probably pointed out the likeness in shapes."

Kate ducked her head, smiling a little.

"She did!" His pink face got pinker. "I can tell by the way you're smiling."

"Don't be so sensitive. Send the message."

Willie was still looking at the picture. "Is this why you thought I was sending the messages? Because this unfortunate *shape* was like mine?"

"No. Send the message."

"How old is he? Did he say? Maybe that's middle-age spread."

"He's probably our age. Send the message."

"A teenage alien? What's he coming down here for— acne treatments? Physoderma?"

"Send the message!"

Willie turned on the computer and typed:

> THIS IS A FRIEND OF THE COMPUTER NUT. I
> AM TRYING TO CONTACT BB-9. ARE YOU
> THERE, BB-9? WILL YOU RECEIVE?

In the silence that followed, Penelope pushed open the door to the kitchen. She stood in the doorway, glaring at them from under her pale bangs.

"No, Penelope, go back," Willie said.

Penelope came forward into the room. She paused at the armchair, out of reach.

"Mom, Penelope's bothering us," Willie called. "Penelope, go back in the kitchen."

"No!"

Penelope's eyes watched the computer. The things that interested her were forbidden things—the telephone, the TV remote control, the computer, the stereo. She walked around the armchair.

"Mom, we're doing homework!" Over his shoulder Willie said to Kate, "I have to tell her that or I have to baby-sit." He turned back to the computer. "I never have a minute to myself, as you may have gathered." He trailed off, his attention on the computer. He typed:

REPEAT. THIS IS A FRIEND OF THE COMPUTER
NUT. I AM TRYING TO CONTACT BB-9. DO YOU
RECEIVE?

He glanced up and said, "Penelope, don't touch anything. I'm not kidding. Hands off!"

Penelope was now beside the computer. Her nose was running, her round eyes watching the keys. She waited for the right moment.

"I mean what I'm saying, Penelope. Go back in the kitchen. Mom, call Penelope!"

On the screen new words were appearing.

THIS IS—

At that moment, with Willie's attention turning back to the screen, Penelope struck. She reached up and clutched as many keys as she could. Her plump fingers squeezed shut. *"Mine!"* she said.

"No! It is *not* yours!"

Willie picked up Penelope, pulling her fingers off the keys.

"Now look what you've done!"

Willie swung Penelope under his arm and carried her, kicking and screaming, into the kitchen.

Kate heard him say, "Mom, now keep Penelope in here, all right? She's really bothering us."

She heard Mrs. Lomax say, "She just wants to be where the action is."

"Mom!"

"Well, put her in the high chair, Willie, and give her some Cheerios."

While Willie was stuffing the unwilling Penelope into her high chair, throwing a handful of Cheerios onto the tray, saying, "There, Attila!" Kate, sitting alone in front of the Apple computer, watched the entire message appear on the screen.

THIS IS BB-9. I AM READY TO RECEIVE YOUR
MESSAGE. GO AHEAD, FRIEND OF THE COM-
PUTER NUT.

The Alien Comedian

For a moment Kate was too stunned to react. Then she slid forward until her hands were on the keyboard. She began to type.

> BB-9, THIS IS THE COMPUTER NUT.

She was hesitating, wondering what to add, when BB-9 began to send a message of his own.

> I AM CONFUSED, COMPUTER NUT. I WAS EX-
> PECTING TO RECEIVE A MESSAGE FROM YOUR
> FRIEND. IS THIS THE SAME FRIEND WHO WAS

WITH YOU LAST TIME? IT IS A DIFFERENT COM-
PUTER.

Kate typed:

NO, THIS IS ANOTHER FRIEND. HIS NAME IS
WILLIE. HOW DID YOU KNOW—

Willie came into the family room and shut the door
behind him. "Sorry about the interruption. Attila the Hun
is now in her high chair, so we shouldn't be interrupted
any more."

HELLO, WILLIE.

Willie stopped as he caught sight of the message on the
computer. "Is that for real?"

WHAT IS IT WILLIE WOULD LIKE TO KNOW?

"He's answered?" Willie asked.
"Yes."
"The teenage alien has answered?" He came forward
a few steps in his worn jogging shoes. "Are you sure you
aren't doing that?"
"No!" Kate held up both hands as a new message appeared on the screen:

REPEAT. I AM READY TO RECEIVE WILLIE'S
MESSAGE. I HAVE NOT GOT, AS YOU SAY, ALL
DAY. PREPARATIONS FOR MY LANDING ARE
TAKING MOST OF MY TIME.

Willie said, "Tell him, for starters, I would like to know where he's from."

Kate typed:

WILLIE WANTS TO KNOW WHAT PLANET YOU
COME FROM.

Willie walked across the room and stood behind Kate's chair. He bent over Kate's shoulder.

I AM FROM THE SOLAR SYSTEM BETELGEUSE,
THE PLANET BAGEL. BAGEL IS THE NINTH
LARGEST PLANET OF THE— WAIT, PERHAPS
YOU WOULD LIKE FOR ME TO DEPICT MY
PLANET.

"By all means," Willie said. "Let's see Bagel."
Kate glanced at Willie and typed:

YES.

"This should be good." Willie pulled up a chair and sat, leaning toward the screen as lines began to appear.

"The planet Bagel. Funneeeeee," Willie said in a disgusted voice as he looked at the completed picture. "And is that supposed to be the moon up there or the hole out of the bagel?"

Kate smiled. "Do you want me to ask him?"

"No, that's exactly what he wants us to do. Ask when he's coming."

Kate typed:

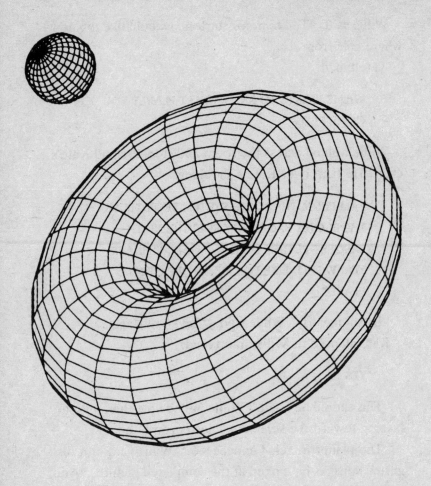

YOU MENTIONED THAT YOU ARE PREPARING
TO LAND ON EARTH. WHEN AND WHERE WILL
YOUR LANDING BE?

The picture of Bagel disappeared.

MY LANDING IS SCHEDULED FOR THURSDAY.
THERE WILL BE A HEAVY FOG THAT NIGHT. I
WILL NEED FOG BECAUSE I WISH TO ARRIVE
UNSEEN. I AM LOOKING AT SEVERAL SITES IN
YOUR AREA.

"Like where?"
Before Kate could type the question, the answer appeared.

ONE POSSIBILITY IS A LARGE RECTANGULAR
FIELD WHICH APPEARS TO BE USED ON FRIDAY
NIGHTS.

"The high school football stadium?" Willie asked. "Is
he considering landing on the football field?"

ALSO UNDER CONSIDERATION IS A LARGE
AREA SOUTH OF THE CITY WHICH IS MARRED
BY THE OCCASIONAL PRESENCE OF FOUR-
LEGGED CREATURES CALLED COWS. I HAVE
HAD BAD LUCK IN THE PAST WITH CREATURES.
I CAN SHOW YOU TOOTH AND FANG MARKS
FROM EVERY PLANET I HAVE VISITED. MY SCAR
FROM CALABRIA IS ESPECIALLY COLORFUL.

"He better go for the cow field," Willie said. "Tell him there's a pep rally on the football field Thursday. Tell him the worst thing cows do is slobber on you, unless of course there's a bull in there. If he sees that one of the cows has horns and—"

"Don't tell me you actually believe this!"

Kate spun around. She spoke unusually harshly because she found that she herself was doing the same thing.

"Well, no, of course I don't believe it. What makes you think I believe it?" Willie pulled back. He crossed his arms and uncrossed them. "He's just got a funny way of putting things, that's all, and half the time he answers questions before we ask them."

Kate and Willie watched each other, measuring the other's gullibility.

It was Willie who broke the silence. "Well, at least go ahead and tell him cows are harmless—just in case, you know."

Kate put her fingers on the keys, but already a new message was appearing.

> NATURALLY THERE WILL BE SOME RISK, NO
> MATTER WHERE I LAND, BUT I AM WILLING TO
> ACCEPT THE ELEMENT OF RISK BECAUSE OF
> MY MISSION.

"Mission! You didn't tell me he had a mission."

"I didn't know."

"Ask him what—wait a minute, let me ask him."

The rest of the message appeared before Willie could get his hands on the keyboard.

> ALL MY LIFE, COMPUTER NUT, I HAVE SUF-
> FERED FROM AN URGE TO LAUGH. LAUGHING
> IS, I BELIEVE, AN ABILITY WE HAD ONCE ON
> MY PLANET, BUT THROUGH LONG PERIODS OF
> DISUSE, WE LOST IT. THIS IS THE SAME WAY
> YOU HUMANS LOST YOUR TAILS. YOU PROBA-
> BLY DO NOT MISS YOUR TAILS, PERHAPS THEY
> WERE EVEN A NUISANCE WHEN YOU STARTED
> WEARING TROUSERS. HOWEVER, I DO MISS
> LAUGHING.

Kate and Willie sat without moving. The kitchen door opened behind them. Penelope came slowly into the room. Unnoticed she crossed the carpet and stood beside Kate. She opened her hand and offered Kate a handful of dirty Cheerios.

> OF COURSE THERE IS NO WAY OF KNOWING
> HOW HUMOROUS I WOULD BE CONSIDERED
> ON EARTH. SINCE NO ONE LAUGHS ON OTHER
> PLANETS, I HAVE HAD NO ACTUAL EXPERIENCE
> IN EVOKING LAUGHTER. I CANNOT COUNT EL-
> MER'S PROGRAMMED HA-HA'S. SO FAR I HAVE
> SUCCESSFULLY AMUSED ONLY MYSELF.

Kate glanced down at the Cheerios. Absently she reached to take one.

"No! Mine!" Penelope clenched her fist around the dirty Cheerios. She waited with her fist beneath her chin. When Kate turned back to the computer, her mouth pulled down with disappointment.

> I AM PREPARING TO SIGN OFF NOW. I HAVE
> MUCH TO DO. THE NEXT TIME I CONTACT
> YOU, COMPUTER NUT, PERHAPS IT WILL BE IN
> PERSON. BB-9 LOGGING.

The Right Side of the Paper

Kate was walking home slowly beneath the arch of tree branches. The leaves overhead blazed with color. Beyond, the October sun was low in the sky, a small copper circle, an hour from disappearing. Kate stared straight ahead, wide-eyed, at nothing.

Swirling in her mind were all the events of the afternoon, of the past days. None of it made sense.

"All right, here's what we'll do," Willie had said finally. "We'll take a sheet of paper and divide it in half, like this." Carefully he folded the sheet of paper and opened it. "Now, on the left-hand side we will put all the reasons we think BB-9's a fake. On the right-hand side the reasons we think he's real—my dad taught me to make decisions like this. Then we look the two lists over realistically and make a decision. It usually works."

He readjusted himself on the sofa. "Well, sometimes it works. One time I made a list of all the reasons I should or should not lose weight, and on the left-hand side were things like 'Being thin is healthy,' and 'Thin people live longer,' and on the right-hand side the reasons I should not lose weight were (A) Hershey bars, (B) hot buttered popcorn, (C) banana splits, and by the time I got to (D) I was so hungry I went in the kitchen and pigged out on Oreos. Well, anyway, let's give it a try."

Kate had been sitting on the sofa, her feet curled under her. BB-9's last words were still pounding in her brain:

> THE NEXT TIME I CONTACT YOU, COMPUTER
> NUT, PERHAPS IT WILL BE IN PERSON.

"Now. (A) Number One. Why do we think he's a fake?" Willie waited. When Kate did not answer, he looked at her closely. "Are you going to do this with me or not?"

"Do what?"

"Make the lists! What do you think I've been talking about for the last half hour? Well, I'll start. We think he's a fake because . . ." He trailed off. His eyes closed in concentration. Then they opened. "Well, frankly, I was not impressed by the Bagel planet, were you?"

"That was a joke. He says he's a sort of amateur comedian."

"Amateur is right. So then why *do* we think he's a fake? Other than that it couldn't possibly happen. I mean, I do not believe in UFOs and aliens and time warps, do you?"

"Yes."

"It seems we can't agree on anything." He scratched his head with his pen. "All right, let's skip the reasons we think he's a fake and move over to the right side of the page. Why do we think he's for real?"

Willie clicked his ballpoint pen open and shut thoughtfully. "(A) Because he has proved to us that he has access to all computers. How about that?" He began to write.

"No, not *all* computers," Kate said, sitting up straighter. "He has access to *two* computers, yours and my dad's. Let's be accurate."

"By all means. Access to *two* computers. How about (B) Because he sometimes answers our questions before we ask them?"

"No, my sister does that all the time."

"So does my mom. She reads my mind. I'll be sitting here, reading a book, and she'll say, 'No, Willie, you cannot have a Snickers.' I mean, she knows the exact candy bar I'm thinking about. And the exact quantity! 'No, Willie, you cannot have thirty-seven M & M's.' I'll cross (B) out. My list is beginning to look like my last science test. Help me."

Kate sighed. She pushed her hair behind her ears and watched Willie without speaking.

Willie said, "Well, how about because of the pictures he sent?"

"Anybody could have drawn those."

"*With* the right program. Well, how about because of—" He dropped his list to his lap in sudden disgust. "Oh, this is stupid. We're not getting anywhere."

"I agree."

"Anyway, I don't think you want him to be real."

"Do you?"

"Sure. I'd like to meet somebody from outer space, even if we could never tell anybody. 'Hey, I met a space creature yesterday.' 'Sure you did, pal. Slip right into this nice, comfortable straitjacket—' " He broke off and looked closely at Kate. "Don't you want that to happen?"

"I don't know what I want."

Kate got up and slipped her feet into her shoes. Willie had been settled comfortably on the sofa, ready for a long conversation about the interesting possibilities of BB-9. Now he got quickly to his feet and glanced at his watch. "You're not going? You don't have to go."

"Yes, I do. It's after five."

Willie groaned to himself. "Well, listen, call me if you hear anything or if anything happens."

"Nothing's going to happen."

"I think it will."

The conversation, the unfinished list had left Kate more confused than ever. She walked slowly up the driveway to her house and opened the side door. She paused, her back resting against the doorway.

In the family room she could see her sister. Cassie was reading a magazine to the dog.

"Now, listen to this, Harvey. Pay attention." She was speaking slowly and carefully, as if to a small child. "Now this article in *People* is about a dog. It's about the dog hero of the year. See, there's his picture. His name's Budweiser. I hate names like that. I'm glad you have a people's name. Here's what Budweiser did. His master was in a boat and it overturned— Oh, hi, Kate, I didn't hear you come in."

"I'm not in yet." Kate pulled herself away from the door. "Why are you reading to the dog?"

"Because I like to. It makes more sense than talking to plants. At least he's got ears—haven't you, Harvey?" She pulled at one ear. "Well, dirty ears, but they're ears."

"I broke my promise," Kate said abruptly.

"I knew that the minute I saw you. You look worse than you did last night."

"I feel worse too."

"You want to talk about it?"

"No."

"Then I will go back to reading about Budweiser. And then, Harvey, I'll get the newspaper and read you Snoopy."

Kate closed the door as she went into her room.

A Suspicion

"No, Willie, nothing has happened!" Kate yelled into the phone as soon as she picked it up. It was the fourth time Willie had called since supper. Cassie had even started saying, "I bet it's Willeeeeeeeee," every time the phone rang.

"I know nothing's happened. Give me a break. That's what I called to tell you. I tried to contact BB-9 three times during *That's Incredible* and—by the way, did you watch that?"

"No, Willie."

"A man put live bees on his face. Well, anyway, I tried three times and he did not answer."

Kate sighed. "He said he was busy, Willie. He said he was getting ready to land on earth. Remember?"

"Of course I remember. But then an interesting thought occurred to me. The only time we have ever contacted him was during normal working hours."

"What?"

"I mean, maybe BB-9's somebody who works at a computer, say, during the day. Get it? And just to liven things up around the coffee machine, he decides to pretend to be from outer space." He paused to let his words take effect. When he heard another sigh, he went on quickly, defensively. "Well, have you ever contacted him after five o'clock?"

"No, but I contacted him on Sunday once." She winced, remembering the events of that particular Sunday.

"Well, lots of people work on Sundays," Willie said. "Anyway, it's just something to put on the left-hand side of the page—no contacts after five P.M."

"All right, Willie, put it on the left-hand side of the page!"

Kate slammed down the phone and glared at it. She was suddenly angry. She wished she had never shared BB-9 with Willie, wished—

Kate's father came out of the kitchen. "I'm glad to see my little girl looking so cheerful."

"That's not funny."

"I can see that, hon. You slammed down the phone like you were detonating something."

"I was. Willie Lomax. I wish he would leave me alone."

"No, you don't."

"I do! He's—" Suddenly Kate's look sharpened as she saw her dad was putting on his jacket. "Where are you going?"

"To the office."

"Can I go?"

"Kate, I'm only going to be there five minutes. I just want to check one X-ray."

"That's all I need—five minutes."

Dr. Morrison sighed. "Come on."

Kate sat in the car beside her father, staring into the oncoming headlights. "You look grim," her father said.

"I feel grim."

"You look like that picture of my Great-Grandmother Morrison that your mother won't let me hang."

"All right, is this better?" Kate said. She forced a smile.

"Much."

"I get sick and tired of people telling me I have no sense of humor, I'm too serious, ought to smile more. Somebody ought to invent a pill that makes people go around smiling."

"I think they have, hon, but it's not legal." Dr. Morrison pulled into his parking space. "Now, Kate, I mean it. Five minutes."

"I know. If I can't do it in five minutes, then I can't do it. It's one of those things."

As her father unlocked the door of the office, Kate pushed past him, into the computer room. Without taking off her jacket, she punched the on button and slipped in the disk.

> THIS IS THE COMPUTER NUT. ARE YOU THERE, BB-9?

She waited, drumming her fingers on the table. She looked at her watch, waited as thirty seconds swept past.

> REPEAT. THIS IS THE COMPUTER NUT. ARE YOU THERE, BB-9?

She checked her watch again. The hand ticked off another thirty seconds. "Answer!" she told the computer.

"Did you say something to me?" her father called from the next room.

"No."

Kate looked at her watch. Another thirty seconds. She realized as she sat there, tensely leaning forward, her hands touching the keys, the seconds slipping away, that she really did want an answer. She wanted BB-9 to be real, not some bored computer person in a downtown office.

She put her hair behind her ears. She looked at her watch again.

"I'm ready, Katie!" her father called from the door.

"But I've got another minute! It's only been four. I've been keeping track of the time."

In the outer office her father flicked the lights off and on, off and on.

"Dad!"

Then she stopped speaking, stopped breathing. For at that moment words began to appear on the computer screen.

THIS IS BB-9. WHY IS EVERYONE ATTEMPTING
TO CONTACT ME? I AM AS BUSY AS A ONE-
ARMED OCTOPUS. I NEED EVERY MOMENT TO
GET READY FOR MY LANDING. IT IS NOT, AS
YOU WOULD SAY, A PIECE OF CAKE. EVERY
FIVE MINUTES IT IS BB-9, ARE YOU THERE? BB-9,
ARE YOU THERE? OF COURSE I AM HERE.
WHAT IS IT YOU WANT?

Self-Portrait of BB-9

Kate did not move for a moment. She was charged with emotion. BB-9 had passed the test. She leaned forward, her body as finely drawn as a violin string.

"Katie," her father called.

She did not answer. Along the edge of her senses she heard her father's voice, but all her interest was on BB-9.

"Katie!"

She barely heard her name. Her mouth had gone dry. With fingers that trembled she began to type.

> BB-9, I WAS CALLING YOU BECAUSE I WANTED
> TO MAKE SURE YOU WERE THERE. MY FRIEND

> WILLIE AND I SUSPECTED YOU WERE SOME-
> BODY PLAYING A JOKE ON US. WE SUSPECTED
> THAT YOU WERE SOMEONE WHO HAD ACCESS
> TO A COMPUTER ONLY DURING WORKING
> HOURS.

She waited tensely, hands clasped on her knees, eyes watching the screen.

> NO, I AM NOT PLAYING A JOKE, ALTHOUGH
> ACTUALLY I DID PLAY A JOKE ON YOU ONCE,
> COMPUTER NUT. THIS WAS WHEN I SENT YOU
> MY PICTURE. THAT WAS THE JOKE. THE PIC-
> TURE WAS OF MY MAIN ROBOT—ELMER. I
> HOPE YOU WILL NOT BE OFFENDED THAT OUR
> ROBOTS HAVE HUMAN NAMES WHILE WE OUR-
> SELVES PREFER MORE MEANINGFUL LETTERS
> AND NUMBERS.

Kate typed:

> NO, I AM NOT OFFENDED. I—

"Kate!"

Her father was standing in the doorway of the computer room now, scowling. He waited, hands in his jacket pockets for her to look at him. She threw him a quick glance over her left shoulder and quickly turned back to the computer screen, where a new message from BB-9 was appearing.

ACTUALLY I AM GLAD THAT YOU CONTACTED
ME, COMPUTER NUT, BECAUSE THIS GIVES ME
THE OPPORTUNITY TO GIVE YOU A CORRECT
PICTURE OF MYSELF. I HAVE, FOR MY EARTH
VISIT, ASSUMED THE APPEARANCE OF AN
EARTHLING. IF I DID NOT, I ASSURE YOU I
WOULD NEVER ACCOMPLISH MY MISSION. IN-
STEAD OF LAUGHTER I WOULD HEAR YELLS OF
FRIGHT. IT WOULD BE MORE OF AN
"EXCCUUUSSSSE ME" SITUATION.

"This is why I never want to bring you with me, Kate,"
her father said. "You always say you'll just be five minutes, and then I have to stand and wait for a half hour.
All my life I have had to wait for women, and I'm tired
of it. First it was my mother. My father and I had the
longest talks of our lives in the car waiting for her to come
out of the store. Then it was Becky Warren. I bet I wasted
half my life waiting for her to . . ."

YOU CAN ALSO RECOGNIZE ME BY THE FACT
THAT I WILL BE WEARING, FOR THE OCCA-
SION, A "WILD AND CRAZY GUY" T-SHIRT. YOU
SHOULD HAVE NO TROUBLE SPOTTING ME.
ARE YOU READY TO SEE MY PICTURE NOW?

Kate typed:

YES.

Her father had trailed off when he saw that Kate was not paying any attention to what he was saying. He came into the room. He had never seen Kate like this. Intensity was in the arch of her spine, the stretch of her neck.

He watched over her shoulder as BB-9's self-portrait

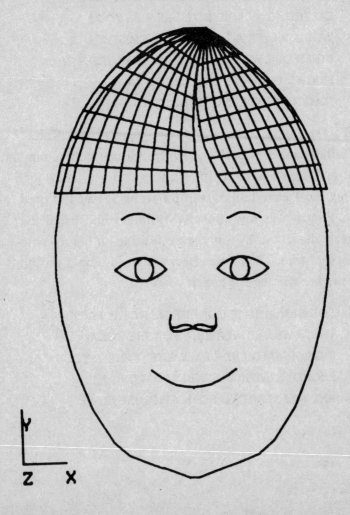

appeared, line by line. When the last detail, the smiling mouth, was in place, he straightened.

"Well, who on earth is that?" he asked.

"It's nobody . . . on *earth*," she answered.

Countdown

"Are you still mad at me?"

"What?"

"Are you still mad?"

Kate looked across the aisle at Linda. Her mind was blank. So much had happened in the past few days that she had forgotten the incident at the office. "Oh, that, no."

"Good. I cannot *stand* for people to be mad at me." Linda flipped open her notebook. "One time when I was real little I dreamed that Mr. Rogers was mad at me and wouldn't let me look in *Picture Picture,* and I woke up in hysterics. My mom thought she was going to have to get a kiddie shrink." Linda pretended to stick her thumb in her mouth. " 'Waaaaaa, Doctor, Mr. Rogers won't let me look in *Picture Picture.*' 'Then you must be a really rotten kid. Get out of here.' So much for my psychoanalysis—"

"Class, may I have your attention, please," the teacher asked, breaking into Linda's monologue.

"Every time Beatenbaugh sees me having a good time, she starts class. Listen, have you done your homework?"

"Half of it."

"Which half? The reading or—I hope—answering the questions? Oh, don't look now, but Willie Lomax is trying to get your attention. If he waves his arms any harder, he'll take off and fly—the Flight of the Bumble Blimp."

"That's mean."

"See, you *are* still mad at me. Whenever you—"

"Linda, may I have your attention along with the rest of the class?"

Linda sighed. "You have my attention, Miss Beaten-baugh."

Kate glanced down at her notebook. She opened it and waited for Miss Beatenbaugh to ask for the homework.

Suddenly the boy on the other side of Kate touched her arm. "This is from Lomax." The boy handed her a piece of notebook paper folded into a small square.

Slowly Kate unfolded the paper and spread it flat on her desk.

I know that something happened after I talked to you last night. I called again and your mom told

me you had gone to the office. Did you contact
BB-9? Did you get him? What did he say??????

Kate sighed. She remembered too clearly sitting in front of the computer with her father leaning over her shoulder. She remembered her father looking at BB-9's picture, asking curiously, "Who's doing that?" She remembered answering, "Someone from outer space."

"Oh, come on, Kate. You don't really believe that."

"It's true! There's no other explanation." She had spun around. "And don't accuse me of making things up, either."

"Oh, Kasie—"

"Don't call me that. You know I hate it. Next you'll start in on Santa Claus and the Easter Bunny."

Her father was silent for a moment, looking down at her. His eyes were thoughtful.

"And don't look at me like that."

"I'll tell you what the trouble is, Kate. You kids today think the world's not interesting enough. You have to make up space invasions and UFOs in order to have some excitement.

"To me, the world is amazing enough without all this E.T. business. Go scuba diving with me sometime and then tell me the world's not an amazing place. Go bird watching with me next Sunday morning. You'll—"

"Dad, I am not making this up."

"Maybe you really don't think you are. I remember when I was a little boy I was absolutely convinced that there was—"

"I know! That there was something hiding in the back of your closet," Kate finished for him. "This is—"

"I actually *saw* something back there one time. Nobody believed me, but it had green eyes and—"

"—and a nose like Porky Pig. Dad, you told me that a hundred times. This is different."

"Your Aunt Helen used to have to go in my closet and look behind my clothes before I could go to sleep. It was as real to me as that computer there."

"Dad, *this is different!*"

Kate broke off, seeing the set expression on her father's face, knowing she could not get behind it. She turned back to the computer. Her face was flushed.

In a blur she saw the words appearing on the video screen. She blinked twice before she could read them.

COMPUTER NUT, TELL YOUR FATHER THAT,
YES, THERE REALLY IS A BB-9. I AM NOT LIKE
THE CREATURE BEHIND HIS CHILDHOOD
CLOTHES. TELL HIM I AM FOR REAL, AS YOU
EARTHLINGS SAY. TELL HIM THAT SOON I WILL
PROVE IT TO HIM.

Kate's father bent over her head. He stared in fascination at the message. Kate could feel his breath parting her hair.

"How are you doing that?"

"I'm not." She held up her hands.

"Oh, I get it. The person you're in contact with is pre-

tending to be from outer space, and you are pretending
to believe him."

"Something like that."

"There's more," her father said.

> I AM NOW STARTING THE COUNTDOWN. IT IS
> TOUCHDOWN MINUS TWENTY AND—AS YOUR
> EARTHLING ASTRONAUTS SAY—COUNTING.

"Whoever it is has a wonderful imagination. But how
did he know about the creature in the back of my closet?"

"Maybe," Kate said as she turned off the computer,
"they are from the same planet."

Kate glanced across the classroom, and her eyes focused
on Willie's face. She watched as he mouthed the words,
"Did you contact him?"

"Yes."

"Did he answer?"

"Yes."

"Meet me after school."

T Minus Five

IT IS NOW T MINUS FIVE . . . AND COUNTING.

It was three o'clock in the afternoon. Outside a light rain had started to fall. Mist was rising from the wet trees, dimming the dark afternoon sky.

Kate and Willie had rushed from school to Willie's house. They now sat in front of his Apple computer, watching the message appearing on the screen.

DID YOU RECEIVE THAT, COMPUTER NUT? T
MINUS FIVE?

"T minus five—that means he's coming tonight, at eight o'clock!"

Kate nodded. Slowly she began to unsnap her jacket.

"I mean, we are no longer talking about some vague, next-month kind of thing." Willie's voice rose. "We are talking about tonight!"

"I know that, Willie."

"Well, you're sitting there with this calm, I-meet-aliens-every-day look on your face. What are we going to do? What are we going to say? What are we— What did your dad say about all this? He was at the office last night, wasn't he?"

"My dad thinks I am making it up. He absolutely refuses to even consider the possibility that BB-9 might be for real."

"That's because of his age. Your dad's too old. So is mine. We—"

Willie broke off as he saw a new message appearing.

I WILL NOT REVEAL THE EXACT POSITION OF
MY LANDING.

"I was afraid of something like this," Willie muttered suspiciously.

THIS IS MY USUAL PRACTICE. SOMETIMES I DO
NOT LIKE WHAT I FIND. THEN I CAN GO,
EXCCUUUSSSSE ME!, AND NO ONE CAN STOP
ME.

Now Kate came to life. She leaned forward and typed:

THEN HOW WILL WE GET TO SEE YOU? WHERE
CAN WE MEET?

"It should be someplace sort of public," Willie said in
a low voice. "I'm not thinking exactly of our safety, but
we don't want to—"

IS BURGER'S PUBLIC ENOUGH FOR YOU?

"Well, Burger's is pretty public," Willie said. "Also, if
he doesn't show, we can have a Nacho-Burger. I love
them."

Kate typed:

BURGER'S IS FINE.

BB-9's message continued.

I WILL MEET YOU THERE AT 20:00. WILL THERE
BE ANY PROBLEM IN THAT HOUR?

"Not for me," Willie said.

NO PROBLEM.

Kate and Willie waited, hunched forward, breathing
like one person. "Do you think he's gone?" Willie asked.

NO, WILLIE, THERE IS ONE THING MORE. DO
NOT BRING ANY OTHER HUMANS WITH YOU.
ALSO NO DOGS OR CATS. EVEN THE MOST
DOCILE OF CREATURES—THE EARTHWORM,

THE BABY DUCK—CAN ATTACK. CREATURES
ARE NOT FOOLED BY APPEARANCES. THEY
KNOW ALIENS AND DO NOT TRUST THEM. IS
THAT AGREED?

"I promise not to bring any earthworms or baby ducks,"
Willie said. "*Or* fleas," he added with a sideways glance
at Kate.

Kate smiled. She typed:

AGREED.

They waited for a moment, and then Willie said, "I
guess that's it." He turned to Kate. "All right, let's make
our plans. I'll tell my mom that I'm going over to your
house to study. I have to do that. If I told her I was going
to Burger's to meet an alien, she'd say, 'You will make
up any excuse, however flimsy, won't you, to get out of
staying with your sisters.' "

Kate looked at him, her head turned to the side. "Do
you really think he's going to show up?"

"I think somebody will. I tell you what. We'll look him
over from outside and then decide if we want to proceed."

"I'll want to proceed," Kate said firmly.

Kate walked into the kitchen and stopped by the counter.
"What are all the balloons for?"

"Didn't I tell you? I'm having a birthday party for Harvey.
He is four years old today."

"Cassie, that's stupid."

"Maybe, but it's cheering me up. Did I tell you? Remember that boy I hugged at the football game? The one that was taking me to the pep rally? He's got the flu."

Cassie was dealing out party favors around the table—dog biscuits tied with ribbons, and party hats with holes for the ears. She stepped back to view the table.

"That's too bad," Kate said. "Who's coming to the party?"

"The guests include Mr. Pop—that's Martee's beagle—and Minna's bringing her poodle. A small, intimate group. The refreshments will be cheeseburgers and Gaines-Burgers. I wanted to get some of that new soda pop for dogs, but Kroger's didn't have any."

"Kroger's just went up in my opinion."

"Don't be so negative. Mom won't be here—she's playing bridge—and—"

"I won't be here either. I'm going to Burger's."

Kate turned. Harvey was sitting by the stove, watching with interest as Cassie adjusted the dog favors. He had already—as a pre-party treat—been allowed to smell his gifts, and he knew he was getting a rubber Hershey bar and a toy that squeaked. He had not yet guessed that it was a frog.

"Happy birthday, Harve."

Kate bent and rubbed him between the ears. Then she straightened and walked down the hall to her room. She tossed her books on the bed.

She stood for a moment looking out the window at the mist swirling around the trees. That feeling rose up her spine.

She lowered her head and brought her watch into focus. T minus three . . . and counting.

The Dog's Birthday Party

The doorbell rang, and Cassie sang out, "Party people, Harvey!" in a cheerful voice. She glanced at her watch. "And they are earleeeeeee!" She was wearing an apron with Snoopy on the pocket.

She opened the door, and when she saw Willie Lomax standing on the porch, her smile faded. "Oh, it's you."

"Sorry to be such a disappointment." Willie waited awkwardly on the welcome mat to be invited inside.

"I just thought you were going to be one of the dogs invited to Harvey's party."

Willie swallowed. "No, I guess I'm a dog who wasn't invited." He slipped into the hallway. "Is Kate ready?"

He pulled the door shut behind him. "We were going to do homework."

"In Burger's?"

"Sort of an assignment . . ." He trailed off. He could lie to his mother with ease, but girls were another matter. He waited, red-faced, against the door.

The doorbell rang, and he jumped as if he'd been poked. Quickly he stepped out of the way.

"Now, this *has* to be party people, Harvey." Cassie swung open the door and looked into the face of a Great Dane. She screamed and put one hand over her heart.

"It's me," Martee shouted. "Mr. Pop couldn't come, so I borrowed Heidi."

"Martee, you cannot bring a Great Dane into my house. Martee, he's bigger than we are."

"She."

"*She.* The invitation was for Mr. Pop." Cassie turned to Willie in her distress. "Mr. Pop is a beagle."

"Mr. Pop had to go to the vet. He has rubbed half the fur off his back. Where do you want Heidi to go?"

"Home!"

"Cassie, you're going to hurt her feelings."

"Well, I don't— Oh, come on in. Take her back to the kitchen. Excuse us, Willie."

"Surely."

He flatted himself against the wall to let Heidi pass, and the dog rolled big, gentle eyes in his direction. "Have a nice time," he told her. He looked up with relief as Kate entered the room. "Your sister's having a party for dogs."

"I know."

In the kitchen Cassie said, "Of *course* the hat doesn't fit. It's meant for a beagle!"

"I hope I'll be in college by the time my sisters are into stuff like this. I'm not a strong person."

Kate nodded. "Me either." She opened the door, and they stepped onto the porch.

It was a cold, still evening. Mist swirled around the trees, turning the yard into a place of graveyard eeriness. Overhead there was no moon or stars.

"Well, he was right about one thing," Willie said. "The visibility is poor."

Kate turned up the hood of her jacket. "Yes, he was right about that."

Willie and Kate were walking rapidly down the sidewalk. The smell of wet leaves and soaked earth filled the air. Drops of water as large as marbles dripped from the trees. An occasional car squished toward town.

Willie was talking constantly. He illuminated the situation for Kate, telling her what he thought, what he was worried about, how he would handle the media if the worst happened and someone reported the landing. He paused occasionally to punch the button on his digital watch and read the numbers aloud.

Kate said nothing. She walked with her hands in her jacket pockets. Her eyes stared straight ahead at the slick pavement.

It was a strange evening, Kate thought—a dog birthday party with favors and an alien at Burger's. And yet neither event—Kate was becoming surer of this by the minute—was going to live up to the hopes for it.

That was the trouble with life—it never quite fulfilled its promises. The wrong dog showed up for the party. The alien didn't show up at all.

Kate raised her head as they rounded the corner. Beyond was the long stretch of overlighted businesses—Long John Silver's, Pizza Hut, the 7-Eleven convenience store, Burger's. The huge golden hamburger on top turned eerily in the distance.

Willie checked his watch. "Two minutes to eight."

Now Kate could see Burger's playground. It, too, looked strange tonight. The top of the Big Burger tree house was lost in the mist. Fog curled around the Nacho-Burger slide and rested on the empty seats of the Double Cheese Choo-choo.

"The parking lot's almost full!" Willie cried in sudden dismay. "What are all these people doing here?"

"Maybe they're eating."

Willie stumbled as he stepped onto the curb. "Or maybe they heard he was coming, somehow. Maybe the news got out. Maybe BB-9 will come, see all the people, and think we told. Maybe he's already left."

Willie made an effort to bring his voice into normal speaking range before he continued. "Maybe he's outside somewhere, hiding like we were going to do." He glanced around the parking lot.

Kate kept walking.

"Anyway, I know he won't be inside, not with all these people. I am beginning to have a very unfortunate feeling about this whole thing, aren't you?"

Without answering, Kate lifted her hand to the door.

Burger's Meeting

"There he is! There he is!" Willie cried. He grabbed Kate's arm.

"Where?"

"At the corner table. The guy by himself. See? Right behind the tray return."

"It looks like him."

Kate stepped sideways, out of the way, to let some people enter. She reached for the door again, but Willie pulled her back. "What are you doing?"

"Going inside."

"Don't rush it. I mean, look at the guy. He's perfectly normal."

"That's how he said he'd look, Willie. He said he was going to take on human form. He said he'd have on a 'Wild and Crazy Guy' T-shirt."

"Sure, human form, but weird human form."

"Antennas coming out of his forehead?"

"No, just something weird—maybe an odd skin color—"

"Green?"

"I don't *know* exactly. It just seems to me that no matter how good he is at taking on human form, there has *got* to be something to give him away, and I don't see anything. This guy is absolutely normal. In fact I think I've seen him around. I think he goes to Hannah Junior High."

Kate pushed at the door, and again Willie drew her back. "Look, Kate, if he *is* playing a joke on us, then he's probably got some of his friends around to enjoy the fun. Look, there they are! See in the middle! Those boys are going to help him make us look like idiots. It will be all over school tomorrow that we went to Burger's to meet an alien."

"I don't care. I'm going inside. I cannot believe that you walked all the way over here to stand outside in the fog."

"I didn't. I just don't want to rush in like an idiot and say, 'Oh, hi, are you the little alien from outer space?'"

"Well, you can stand out here all night, but I am going in."

This time Kate didn't give him a chance to stop her. She pushed opened the door, dodged a man emptying trash into the bin, passed the lines at the counter, and walked directly through the lines of tables to where the boy sat.

The boy was sitting quietly, looking down at his tray. On it was an unopened cheeseburger, unopened Coke, unwrapped straw. Yet somehow Kate got the feeling he was the center of attention at Burger's.

She glanced around. Some people were staring with open curiosity at him. Some glanced at him sideways as they ate. Others watched his reflection in the mirror.

"Hi," Kate said. Her mouth had gone dry.

The boy looked up at her with pale eyes. His lips drew back into a small smile.

"I'm Kate—you know, the computer nut." She paused and then went on in a rush. "My friend Willie's waiting outside. He's not sure if you're for real or not, and he's afraid you are going to make fools of us. He's—"

She broke off in quick embarrassment. Two spots of color appeared high on her cheeks. "Have I got the right person? You *are* BB-9, aren't you? I mean, I just assumed you were because you look like your picture and because of the T-shirt and—"

YOU ARE LIKE YOUR PICTURE TOO. I WOULD HAVE KNOWN YOU ANYWHERE.

Kate leaned down abruptly, her hands braced on the table. Her hair fell forward around her face. Her dark eyes were intent. "Say that again?"

> I SAID THAT YOU ARE LIKE YOUR PICTURE ALSO. WHAT IS THE TROUBLE WITH EVERYONE AROUND HERE? WHY AM I ASKED TO REPEAT EVERYTHING? IS MY VOICE ALARMING?

"No, it's not alarming. It just sounds, sort of—well, mechanical."

> THE TROUBLE, COMPUTER NUT, IS THAT AL-THOUGH WE CAN DUPLICATE THE APPEAR-ANCE OF THE HUMAN BODY, WE CANNOT DUPLICATE HUMAN SPEECH. WE CAN ONLY RE-PRODUCE IT. DO I SOUND LIKE ONE OF YOUR COMPUTERS? IS THIS WHY EVERYONE IS STAR-ING AT ME?

"You do sound a little like a computer, but it doesn't bother me at all," she said in a rush. "It's fine, really."

Kate glanced over her shoulder, wishing that Willie would come in. Through the mist on the door, she saw his round face, watching them.

> IT IS OBVIOUSLY NOT FINE. I AM AN OBJECT OF CURIOSITY. PERHAPS THAT IS WHY I HAVE HAD NO SUCCESS SO FAR IN MAKING PEOPLE LAUGH.

Kate cleared her throat. "You've already tried?"

MANY TIMES. I COULD NOT RESIST. FIRST I
WENT UP AND GOT IN LINE TO PLACE MY
ORDER. AS I WAITED I PREPARED A SMALL
JOKE. I SAID TO THE WAITRESS, WHAT IS LIT-
TLE, GREEN AND GOES ERRRRRRP? I SAID A
MARTIAN WITH INDIGESTION. THE WAITRESS
SAID, IS THAT A JOKE? I SAID, IS A SPACE DOG
FROM THE BARK SIDE OF THE MOON?
SHE SAID, WOULD YOU TELL MYRTLE A JOKE?
I SAID, SURE, BRING HER OVER.
MYRTLE CAME. I SAID, MYRTLE, HOW DOES A
CREATURE FROM THE PLANET RYS TELL TIME?
WITH HIS RYS WATCH.
MYRTLE DID NOT LAUGH EITHER. SHE ASKED,
IS THERE SOMETHING WRONG WITH YOUR
THROAT? I SAID, YES, I HAVE A FROGONIAN
IN IT. AGAIN NO LAUGHTER.
PERHAPS MYRTLE DID NOT KNOW
FROGONIANS ARE SMALL CREATURES
WITH ODD VOICES WHO COME FROM THE
PLANET FROGO.

"I'm sure she didn't know what a Frogonian is. I don't.
That's too far out for around here."

REALLY? WELL, THEN MYRTLE SAID, WOULD
YOU TELL MIKE A JOKE?

I SAID, SURE, BRING HIM OVER.
I SAID, MIKE, HOW MANY VOYKINS DOES IT
TAKE TO WASH A SPACE SHUTTLE?
TWO, ONE TO HOLD THE SPONGE AND ONE
TO DRIVE THE SHUTTLE BACK AND FORTH.

"Did he laugh?"

I REGRET TO SAY MIKE DID NOT FIND THAT
HUMOROUS. PERHAPS HE DID NOT KNOW
THAT VOYKINS ARE KNOWN THROUGHOUT THE
UNIVERSE FOR THEIR LACK OF BRILLIANCE.

"I didn't know it." Kate glanced at the door and beck-
oned Willie to come in.

IF THAT IS TRUE, MY NEXT SERIES OF JOKES
WAS ALSO DOOMED TO FAIL.

"What were they?"

A VOYKIN CAN TELL UP FROM DOWN ONLY IF
YOU GIVE HIM TWO GUESSES. AND THEN I
FOOLISHLY TRIED, HOW CAN YOU TELL A VOY-
KIN SPACESHIP? IT'S THE ONE WITH TRAINING
WHEELS.

"I think that's funny."

REALLY? YOU AREN'T JUST SAYING THAT TO
MAKE ME FEEL BETTER?
BECAUSE I WAS DESPERATE, I LAPSED

INTO POOR TASTE AND SAID, HOW MANY VOY-
KINS DOES IT TAKE TO GET A DRINK OF
WATER ON EARTH? TWO, ONE TO DRINK AND
ONE TO HOLD UP THE TOILET LID.

"Oh, dear."

THAT IS EXACTLY WHAT MYRTLE SAID. SHE
AND MIKE WENT BACK TO WORK. THE WAIT-
RESS GAVE ME MY CHEESEBURGER. I WENT TO
MY TABLE.

"I am so sorry, BB-9."

ME TOO.

Have You Heard
This One?

"So those were the only jokes you had a chance to try?"

OH, NO. WELL, I SHOULD HAVE STOPPED
THERE. THE SMELL OF FAILURE WAS
STRONGER THAN THE SMELL OF FRENCH
FRIES, BUT ON THE WAY TO MY TABLE I DE-
CIDED TO HAVE ANOTHER, AS YOU SAY,
CRACK AT IT. I STOPPED AT THE FIRST TABLE.
I SAID, WHAT DO YOU GET WHEN YOU BLOW
UP THE PLANET ENDOR?
ENDUST. NO LAUGHTER.
I STOPPED AT THE SECOND TABLE.

I SAID, WHAT DO YOU GET WHEN YOU BLOW
UP THE PLANET LYT?
LYTTER.
NO LAUGHTER. NOT EVEN A SMILE.
I STOPPED AT THE THIRD TABLE.
I SAID, WHAT DO YOU GET WHEN YOU BLOW
UP THE PLANET DANDOR?
DANDRUFF.
BY NOW EVERYONE WAS LOOKING AT ME AND
NOT IN A HUMOROUS WAY. I BEGAN TO THINK
MY JOKES MIGHT BE TOO VIOLENT—THAT ALL
THIS BLOWING UP OF PLANETS WAS, AS YOU
WOULD SAY, TURNING THEM OFF.

"No, I think you just took them by surprise. People in Burger's aren't used to comedians coming to their tables to deliver jokes."

OR PERHAPS I SHOULD HAVE TRIED A JOKE
FROM A CLOSER PLANET, ONE THE PEOPLE
WOULD BE FAMILIAR WITH. A PLANET LIKE
GALAXIA, FOR EXAMPLE. GALAXIA IS WELL
KNOWN THROUGHOUT THE UNIVERSE FOR ITS
LARGE, UNAPPEALING WOMEN.

BB-9 spoke thoughtfully, his pale eyes turned upward, toward the ceiling. His voice, mechanical and without inflection, droned in the hushed room.

> HOW DO YOU TELL A GALAXIAN WOMAN
> FROM A HIPPOPOTAMUS?
> THE HIPPOPOTAMUS DOESN'T HAVE ON LIP-
> STICK.

Kate interrupted him. "Let's go outside. Everyone's staring at us and, anyway, I want you to meet Willie." BB-9 got to his feet.

> YES, I AM READY TO LEAVE. I HAVE BEEN ON
> YOUR PLANET FOR ONE HOUR AND I HAVE NOT
> LAUGHED OR HEARD ANYONE LAUGH A SIN-
> GLE TIME. ON SLIMOVIA I WAS SLITHERING
> AROUND LIKE A NATIVE FIVE MINUTES AFTER
> MY SPLASHDOWN. I AM NOT USED TO FAIL-
> URE.

"This way."

Kate took BB-9 by the arm, and he was cool to the touch, his skin smooth, hairless. As they walked to the door, BB-9 began to speak again. Every person at the counter turned to listen.

> PERHAPS YOU ARE RIGHT IN WHAT YOU SAID.
> PERHAPS MY HUMOR IS TOO FAR OUT. I
> SHOULD BE MORE TERRESTRIAL IN MY AP-
> PROACH, GIVE THE PEOPLE SOMETHING THEY
> CAN, AS YOU SAY, RELATE TO.

He straightened his shoulders. The lines of discourage-ment eased from his forehead.

> YES, NEXT TIME I WILL BE MORE PERSONAL.
> YOU HAVE BEEN OF GREAT HELP TO ME. FROM
> NOW ON MY JOKES WILL DEFINITELY BE MORE
> PERSONAL.

Willie was waiting just outside the door. "Willie," Kate said, "this is BB-9, and he is for real."

BB-9 looked at Willie. His smile drew the corners of his mouth up.

> GLAD TO MEET YOU, WILLIE.
> MY, YOU ARE FAT.
> I BET YOU GET FAN MAIL FROM ELEPHANTS!

He turned to Kate, his face bright.

> WAS THAT BETTER, COMPUTER NUT? OR
> WOULD IT HAVE BEEN FUNNIER TO SAY, MY,
> YOU ARE SO FAT I BET IN YOUR GRADUATION
> PICTURE YOU WERE THE FRONT ROW!

Willie stepped back against the side of the building. Kate, seeing the stunned, hurt look on his face, stepped quickly between them. "BB-9, you—"

> DON'T STOP ME NOW, COMPUTER NUT. I AM
> ON A ROLL.
> ON THE BEACH, WILLIE, DO PEOPLE PAY TO
> SIT IN YOUR SHADE?
> NOW I AM GETTING THE HANG OF IT. WILLIE, I
> BET YOU HAVE YOUR OWN ZIP CODE.

BB-9 spun around to take in the rest of the parking lot. His pale eyes gleamed as he caught sight of two ladies getting out of a Ford.

HEY, LADY! YOU ARE SO BOWLEGGED YOU
COULD WALK DOWN A BOWLING ALLEY *DUR-
ING* THE GAME!
AND YOU! YES, THE OTHER ONE. YOU REMIND
ME OF A ROLL OF FILM—UNDERDEVELOPED!

He took a few steps to get a better view of the old man getting out of a pickup truck.

MISTER! OVER HERE! IF YOU WALKED INTO AN
ANTIQUE SHOP, SOMEBODY WOULD TRY TO
BUY YOU!

"I think," Kate said to Willie, "we better get him out of here."

WHY? I AM NOT FUNNY? WHAT IS HAPPENING
WITH THESE UNSMILING PEOPLE?

"I'll tell you about it on the way home," Kate said.
BB-9 pulled down his "Wild and Crazy Guy" T-shirt, and his smile faded. His shoulders sagged.

LET'S GO.

The Laughing Planet

BB-9, Kate, and Willie were crossing the wet, deserted street. BB-9 was saying:

> THIS IS NOT AT ALL AS I IMAGINED. I AM NOW
> NINETY MINUTES INTO MY VISIT, TERRESTRIAL
> TIME, AND NOT ONE SINGLE LAUGH, NO PIES
> IN THE FACE, NO SLIPS ON BANANA PEELS.
> WHAT IS IT WITH THIS PLANET? ALL MY LIFE I
> HAVE DREAMED OF COMING HERE, OF—AS
> YOU WOULD SAY—CRACKING EVERYBODY UP,
> AND I AM AS MISERABLE AS I HAVE EVER BEEN
> ON AN INTERPLANETARY VISIT. I HAVE, TO BE
> BLUNT, LAID AN EGG.

"I know how you feel," Willie said with quick sympathy. "Last year at computer camp I had to emcee the talent show, and after my opening joke everybody groaned."

"Let him finish, Willie."

THANK YOU, COMPUTER NUT. EVEN ON THE
PLANET XEROXAN, WHICH IS KNOWN AS THE
ONION PLANET BECAUSE IF YOU DIG INTO THE
CRUST FUMES COME UP AND MAKE YOU CRY, I
WORE SPIKE SHOES IN AN ATTEMPT TO BE
AMUSING, BUT EVERYBODY, EVEN MYSELF,
WAS SOON IN TEARS, AND I HAD TO GROPE
MY WAY BACK TO THE SHIP—EVEN THERE, I
DID NOT FEEL AS MISERABLE AS I DO HERE. I
THINK IT IS TIME FOR ME TO MAKE A QUICK
EXIT.

"But you can't leave yet!" Kate said.

"You've never bombed, Kate—you don't know how bad it makes you feel."

"Look, BB-9, there's my house. The lights are on in the basement. That means my dad's home. You promised to meet him, remember? This is really important to me. Please!"

"Dr. Morrison's a very nice man," Willie said. "I can't honestly say he's a barrel of laughs, but he—"

DR. MORRISON? YOUR FATHER IS A DOCTOR?

"Yes."

> THEN I WILL COME IN FOR A MOMENT. MEDI-
> CAL AND LABORATORY JOKES ARE ONE OF MY
> SPECIALTIES.

BB-9's back was straight now. He squared his shoulders beneath his T-shirt. He began to smile.

> WHAT HAS ORANGE HAIR, WEARS FUNNY
> SHOES, AND COMES OUT OF A TEST TUBE?
> BOZO THE CLONE.

His smile broadened.

> EVEN ELMER SEEMS TO LIKE MY MEDICAL
> JOKES. HE TURNS UP THE VOLUME ON HIS
> HA-HA'S.
> WHAT DOES A CREATURE FROM ALPHA TAKE
> FOR AN UPSET STOMACH?
> ALPHA SELTZER.
> HOW DOES A VOYKIN SPELL RELIEF? B-U-R-P.

He laughed.

> MEDICAL JOKES BREAK ME UP.
> A MARTIAN COMES TO EARTH AND GOES TO
> THE DOCTOR. THE DOCTOR SAYS, MY, ARE
> ALL MARTIANS GREEN LIKE YOU?
> YES.
> DO ALL MARTIANS HAVE ANTENNAS COMING
> OUT OF THEIR EARS?
> YES.

ARE ALL MARTIANS COVERED WITH LITTLE
RED DOTS?
ONLY THOSE WITH MEASLES.

"This way," said Kate. She opened the door. "Dad?"
"Just a minute."

Dr. Morrison did not glance up. He was in the middle
of his model train set. His trains were speeding around
the H-O gauge track. Electric signals were going up and
down, bells were ringing, station masters were darting in
and out of stations. One train came out of a tunnel and
pulled onto a side track. The other chugged up a papier-
mâché mountain and into the station. Then Dr. Morrison
looked up. "Hello, Kate, Willie."

"And, Dad, this is BB-9."

BB-9 stepped around Kate. He watched Dr. Morrison
with a smile of anticipation. His pale eyes gleamed.

"Remember, Dad, you saw BB-9's picture on the computer? Remember you thought he wasn't real?"

"Oh, yes. Well, I'm glad to see that you are." Dr.
Morrison took off his engineer's cap and stuck out his
hand. "Kate has had a lot of fun out of your communi-
cations. For a while there we thought you were going to
turn out to be a little green man."

BB-9 came forward to take Dr. Morrison's hand.

I ASSUME THE COLOR GREEN ONLY WHEN I
VISIT THE PLANET CHLOROPHYLLIA. I UNDER-
STAND THAT YOU ARE A DOCTOR.

At the mechanical sound of BB-9's voice, Dr. Morrison looked at Kate and then at BB-9 and then back at Kate. A broad smile came over his face.

"Oh, no." He held up his hands. He backed off. "No, you don't. I absolutely refuse to be taken in by this. You are still pretending that this boy is from outer space, right?"

"Listen, Dr. Morrison," Willie said, stepping forward quickly, "this is for real. I didn't believe it myself at first, but—"

"Now, I have to admit, Kate, that you have played this whole thing very carefully, very skillfully. You have led up to this moment perfectly. The voice is a master touch, and if your mother were here, she'd fall for it completely."

"Dad!"

"Dr. Morrison, listen to Kate. She's telling the truth!"

"This is a super practical joke. And it was your idea, wasn't it?" he said, turning to BB-9. "Well, I have to congratulate you."

WHAT DO YOU MEAN, A SUPER PRACTICAL JOKE? WHAT IS HE SAYING, COMPUTER NUT? I HAVE NOT TOLD THE FIRST JOKE YET. DR. MORRISON, HOW MANY PROTOVIAN DOCTORS DOES IT TAKE TO REMOVE AN—

"Wait, I've got an idea. I'll call your mom. She's over at Boo's playing bridge, and it will only take her two minutes—maximum—to get home. She'll fall for this hook, line, and sinker."

WAIT. I THOUGHT OF A BETTER ONE.

BB-9 chuckled.

WHY DO NURSES ON PLOTOVIA WEAR
POINTED HATS?

"Yes, sir, she'll get a real kick out of this." Dr. Morrison paused halfway up the stairs. He leaned over the banister. He said to BB-9, "See, Kate's mom has been worrying about Kate's communicating with you, and she really believes in UFOs. She thought she saw one last summer. I had to stop her from calling the radio station. Now, I won't be a minute."

BUT, SIR, I HAVE TIME FOR ONLY ONE OR TWO
MORE TRIES.
WHY DO THE AMBULANCES ON EXXYOR HAVE
SQUARE WHEELS?

As Dr. Morrison ran up the rest of the steps, two at a time, BB-9 stepped back, closer to the door.

I AM GETTING WORSE. THIS TIME I DID NOT
EVEN GET TO GIVE A SINGLE PUNCH LINE.

"I'd like to hear the punch lines," Willie said. "Why *do* ambulances on Exxyor have square wheels?"

TO KEEP THE PATIENTS FROM—

Suddenly BB-9 stopped. He took two quick steps backward. His thin arms flew up in alarm.

WHAT WAS THAT?

"I don't know what you're talking about," Kate said.

ANIMAL NOISES. THERE ARE ANIMALS IN THIS
HOUSE.

"They're just dogs. My sister's having a birthday party for our dog."

"If you don't act scared," Willie began, "dogs won't—"

IT IS NOT AN ACT.

BB-9 hugged himself in alarm, his hands clutching his thin arms. His pale eyes widened.

I DEPART NOW.

"Not yet, please." Kate sprang forward, but with a speed that was animal-quick BB-9 turned and opened the door. He disappeared instantly into the mist.

"Come on," Willie said, "or we'll lose him." His hand was on the doorknob before the door had a chance to close. Kate was right behind him.

They ran outside and stood, ankle deep, in the mist. They hesitated, and then Willie caught a glimpse of BB-9's white shirt at the curb.

"There he is!"

They joined hands and ran down the driveway.

Five minutes later Kate's father came back down the stairs. "She's on her way," he called cheerfully to the empty basement. "I didn't tell her what was happening, just that we had a big surprise, so when she comes in . . ."

Dr. Morrison trailed off.

He turned to Cassie and the birthday party guests at the head of the stairs. In a voice low with puzzlement he said, "Now, where on earth did they go?"

The Bologu Football

WHAT IS THAT WONDERFUL NOISE?

BB-9 paused suddenly, and Kate and Willie almost ran into him in the mist. They stopped and heard the throbbing beat in the distance of "Bob-cats! Bob-cats! Bob-cats!"

"Oh, that. That's the pep rally," Willie said. "People around here go crazy over football games. That's where you almost made the mistake of landing."

BUT IT SOUNDS LIKE A WONDERFUL CROWD.

BB-9 stood with his head to one side, birdlike, listening to the noise.

"Oh, they're wonderful, all right, until they lose, and then watch out."

BB-9 was still listening. There was a faraway look in his eyes.

NOW I HEAR MUSIC AND SINGING. IT
OCCURS TO ME THAT SUCH A CHEERFUL
GROUP WOULD LIKE SOME HUMOR AS
WELL.

"No!" Kate stepped in front of BB-9, blocking his way. "Believe me, a pep rally is no place for you."

"She's right," Willie said.

BUT THE CROWD IS ALREADY—HOW DO YOU
PUT IT?—WARMED UP. I COULD STEP RIGHT IN
WITH A FEW JOKES. WHAT KIND OF EVENT IS
THIS EXACTLY?

"It's football, but, BB-9—"

I LOVE FOOTBALL GAMES, I LOVE THEM. ALL
THAT HUSTLE AND BUSTLE OVER A BROWN
BALL. AND SPORTS JOKES ARE ONE OF MY SPE-
CIALTIES. DIDN'T I TELL YOU? AND WITH SUCH
A CHEERFUL GROUP, HOW COULD I MISS?

"You could miss, BB-9," Kate said.

"Believe her," Willie added.

BUT LISTEN TO THEM.

Again cheers rose from the stadium. The pep song blared
from the band. BB-9 began to walk toward the noise like
a sleepwalker. Kate glanced helplessly at Willie and then
followed.

> AT LEAST LET ME HAVE A LOOK. ON THE WAY I
> WILL TELL YOU A TRUE FOOTBALL STORY. YOU
> WILL, I AM SURE, FIND THIS MOST AMUSING. I
> IMAGINE THE PEP RALLY PEOPLE WILL TOO.

Kate cast a worried look at Willie, and he shrugged.
Between them, unconcerned, BB-9 had begun to smile.

> FIRST OF ALL, LET ME EXPLAIN THAT THE
> CREATURES ON THE PLANET BOLOGU ARE
> VERY SMALL, THAT HIGH, ONE INCH MAX. AND
> THEIR SPACESHIPS LOOK EXACTLY LIKE FOOT-
> BALLS—SAME SIZE, SAME SHAPE, SAME
> COLOR.

BB-9 broke into a laugh.

> I CANNOT HELP BUT CHUCKLE AT THIS MY-
> SELF. YOU WILL HAVE TO FORGIVE ME. THE
> TRUTH IS OFTEN MORE AMUSING THAN MY
> JOKES. ANYWAY, A PARTY FROM BOLOGU
> CAME TO EARTH ON A RECONNAISSANCE MIS-
> SION, AND BY CHANCE THEY FLY OVER PITTS-
> BURGH. THERE THEY SEE A BIG STADIUM, ALL
> LIT UP, LOTS OF PEOPLE, PLENTY OF EXCITE-

MENT. THEY FLY LOWER AND THEY ARE HORRI-
FIED. LO AND BEHOLD, THEY SEE THAT THE
PITTSBURGH STEELERS ARE HANDLING A BO-
LOGU SPACESHIP IN A MOST HEARTLESS MAN-
NER. THEY ARE THROWING IT AROUND,
FIGHTING OVER IT. THEY ARE EVEN KICKING IT
LONG DISTANCES. THE BOLOGU TRY TO CON-
TACT THEIR SISTER SHIP, BUT THEY GET NO
ANSWER. OBVIOUSLY THE BOLOGU ELECTRI-
CAL SYSTEM IS NO LONGER FUNCTIONAL.
THERE IS ONLY ONE THING TO DO—LAUNCH
AN IMMEDIATE RESCUE MISSION. THEY DO
THIS IN THE MIDDLE OF A PLAY SO AS TO TAKE
ADVANTAGE OF THE CONFUSION. TO THEIR
HORROR, ONE OF THE PLAYERS LEAPS INTO
THE AIR, GRABS THEIR SPACESHIP, STUFFS IT
UNDER HIS ARM, AND RUNS DOWN THE FIELD
WITH IT. THE OTHER PLAYERS CHASE HIM, BUT
THEY CANNOT CATCH HIM. THE PLAYER GOES
INTO THE END ZONE, TAKES THE BOLOGU
SPACESHIP AND SPIKES IT.

BB-9 paused and looked at Kate.

SPIKING IS THROWING THE FOOTBALL DOWN
ON ITS END. HARD. LIKE THIS.

BB-9 spiked an imaginary football.

IT WOULD BE A MOST DISRUPTIVE MANEUVER
FOR A SPACESHIP.

Kate said, "I can imagine."
"Me, too," said Willie.
BB-9 wiped tears of laughter from his eyes.

HERE COMES THE FUNNY PART. "TOUCH-
DOWN!" SCREAMS THE CROWD. "TOUCH-
DOWN!" INSIDE THE BOLOGU SHIP, THE CREW
IS STRUGGLING TO THEIR FEET. SOME ARE IN-
JURED. THEY LISTEN TO THE YELLS OF
"TOUCHDOWN." THE CAPTAIN SHAKES HIS
HEAD. "TOUCHDOWN—NO WAY. I WILL NEVER
TOUCHDOWN HERE AGAIN."

BB-9 wiped his eyes. Shaking his head, he turned to
look at Kate. Then at Willie.

YOU ARE NOT LAUGHING? YOU DO NOT FIND
THAT AMUSING?

"Oh, yes, it's amusing, it's very amusing," Kate said.

BUT YOU DO NOT LAUGH. WHEN DO PEOPLE
LAUGH AROUND HERE? THAT IS WHAT I
WOULD LIKE TO KNOW.

"BB-9, I was just listening to it from the viewpoint of
the crowd at the pep rally, that's all."

THE PEP CROWD WOULD NOT FIND IT
AMUSING?

"I don't know. I just—well, nobody tells jokes at pep
rallies. It's not done."

"Pep rallies are to psych everybody up for the game,"
Willie added.

I THINK I GET WHAT YOU ARE SAYING. YOU
THINK THE STORY IS TOO FAR REMOVED
FROM, AS YOU SAY, BOBCAT TERRITORY.

"No, that's not what we're saying."
BB-9 decided not to hear her.

WELL, PERHAPS YOU ARE RIGHT. PERHAPS I
SHOULD TELL A SHORTER, PEPPIER STORY, A
MORE TOPICAL STORY. LET ME
SEE . . . BOBCATS . . . BOBCATS . . .

BB-9's steps quickened as he made his way toward the
cheers.

Pep Rally Posse

WHAT A CHEERFUL SIGHT!

BB-9 and Kate and Willie had just stepped out of the mist. BB-9 was turning slowly in an admiring circle.

Below, the cheerleaders were shaking their pompoms while the band played the Bobcats pep song. The crowd was clapping in time. Then the head cheerleader jumped up and down and yelled, "Look! Here's the captain of the Bobcats—Ronnie Abernathy!"

The crowd roared as Ronnie came forward. He ducked his head. He scratched his shoulder. He said, "Well, I just want to say, uh, that we're all going to give one hundred and twenty percent tomorrow night, and we hope you'll all be, uh, real proud of us."

"Yaaaaaaahhhhhhhhhh, Ronnnnnnnnnnie, go get 'em!"

BB-9 was smiling. He was as fascinated as a kid at Disney World. He moved down the embankment and around the bleachers. He stepped onto the field.

"Stop him, Willie," Kate pleaded. She was wringing her hands.

"I don't think we can. All we can do is stick around." He swallowed. "And pick up the pieces."

He grabbed her hand, and they followed BB-9 to the field.

BB-9 walked to where the cheerleaders had started making a pyramid of themselves. He admired it for a moment. He had never seen such a thing on any other planet. When the pyramid broke out of formation into a jumble of cartwheels and somersaults, he applauded with the crowd. Then he turned and held up both hands for silence. It seemed a good time for a joke.

"Who *is* that?" someone in the crowd muttered. "What's he doing on the field?"

"It's probably an announcement. Maybe somebody left their car lights on."

EARTHLING STUDENTS, LADIES AND
GENTLEMEN.

The cheerleaders stepped back, looking at BB-9, waiting. His voice had the official, microphone sound they respected. They stood the way they stood during the national anthem, heads up, arms at their sides, pompoms lowered.

YOU ARE PROBABLY WONDERING WHO I AM
AND WHAT I AM DOING AT YOUR PEP RALLY.

He smiled.

WELL, THE TRUTH IS THAT I AM A VISITOR TO
EARTH, FROM ANOTHER GALAXY.

Kate groaned beneath her breath. "This is awful, Willie." She took his arm again for support. "Genuinely awful."

"I know." Willie shook his head from side to side, regretfully, helplessly, one friend watching another go down the tube.

"I feel so sorry for him."

I AM ON A MISSION, A SORT OF HUMOROUS
MISSION.

"What did he say he was on?"

Now most of the people were looking around, seeking a reason for the disruption.

"Did he say he was a visitor to earth?"

"That's what it sounded like to me."

"Where's he got his microphone hidden?"

"He looks like he's on some sort of drugs, doesn't he to you?"

"If it's an announcement, I wish he'd get on with it."

AND NOW FOR MY FIRST JOKE.

"Joke? *Joke!*"

The word swept through the crowd, rippling down the rows. Then a silence fell over the bleachers. It was the kind of silence that usually came when "Refrigerator" Morris missed a key block and the other team scored.

One mother, kinder than the others, said, "He's probably being initiated into some club and they're making him do this."

"Well, they shouldn't do this at pep rallies. Let them take up school time with initiations."

"I agree."

BB-9 looked at the silent crowd with the first sign of uneasiness. He tugged at his "Wild and Crazy Guy" T-shirt. He crossed his arms over his chest.

WELL, HERE GOES.

His voice sounded suddenly high and reedy in the October night air.

THERE WAS THIS FOOTBALL TEAM CALLED THE BOBCATS.

As soon as he said, "Bobcats," the cheerleaders yelled, "Yeah, Bobcats!" They jumped up and did splits in the air. There were a few cartwheels. The word "Bobcats" did this to them. It was as if they were programmed to explode every time they heard it. "Yeah, Bobcats!"

Now the cheerleaders, in their excitement, moved in front of BB-9. BB-9 pushed his way through arms and legs and pompoms and cleared his throat. This turned up the volume on his voice.

SO THESE BOBCATS WERE—

"Yeah, *Bobcats*!"

Now the crowd took it up. *"Bob-cats! Bob-cats! Bob-cats!"* The word caused its usual chain reaction, and soon every person—except Willie and Kate—was shouting, "Bobcats!"

BB-9 would not give up. Again he cleared his throat.

AND THE BOBCATS WERE GETTING READY FOR
THEIR GAME WITH THE SENECA INDIANS.

The crowd stopped chanting "Bobcats" just in time to hear BB-9 shout "Seneca Indians." They did not like what they heard. The comments that now rippled through the crowd were less friendly in tone.

"Did he say he's *for* the Seneca Indians?"

"That's what it sounded like to me."

"I knew he looked funny."

"That's because he's from Seneca."

"Did you hear that? He's from Sennnnnecaaaaa!"

As that word rang through the stands, two boys in the front row got to their feet. The football team got up too. Refrigerator Morris was in front, in his usual crouch.

BB-9 took one step back.

Up in the bleachers a group of fans rose and started down, climbing over people to get to the field and BB-9. There was a murmur of encouragement as people helped boost them forward.

"We've got to get him out of here," Kate said.

She darted forward, through the startled cheerleaders, and grabbed BB-9's arm. He was standing there, staring with a kind of horrible fascination at the people closing in on him.

"Come on!"

BUT WHAT DID I DO? WHAT DID I—

"Now!"

Kate spun BB-9 around, and they started across the field, running for the players' exit. Kate had her head down, but she could hear the shouts of people behind them, hitting the field, beginning the chase.

"This way," Kate said as they got to the gate.

Behind them Willie gasped, "Go ahead, I'll try to lead them around the gym." He jabbed his thumb in the other direction.

He leaned against the gate to catch his breath. As the first of the crowd broke through the fog, he straightened. "They went that way! Hurry! That way!"

Arm outstretched, he watched as the crowd poured through the gate.

"That way!" he told the second wave of people.

Like cattle on a stampede, they roared around the school gym and into the mist beyond.

Willie waited by the gate, listening to the shouts of confusion in the distance.

"Where did they go?"

"This way."

"No, over here."

"Come on! They must have cut through the parking lot!"

When Willie heard the shouts fading away, he turned and started running after BB-9 and Kate.

Good-bye

The next ten minutes were hectic for BB-9 and Kate. Kate had no idea whether the crowd was behind them or not. She kept running through the fog with BB-9 in the lead. They ran down streets, through yards, cut through gas stations, parking lots. Now they were on grass, now asphalt, now weeds.

They moved farther away from the city. Now they ran through fields, climbed fences, dodged trees. A cow mooed in the distance, and BB-9 clutched her hand tighter.

Then they ducked under the low limbs of a tree and came to a halt in a small clearing. BB-9 stood with his head to one side, listening. In the silence the only thing

Kate could hear was the pounding of her own heart.

BB-9 turned to face her.

> IT WOULD NOT BE SAFE FOR YOU TO ACCOM-
> PANY ME FARTHER—THE BLAST-OFF, YOU
> KNOW. WE WILL SAY GOOD-BYE HERE.

"But will I ever hear from you again?" Kate asked. She felt that something was going out of her life, something she would not be able to replace.

BB-9 smiled crookedly.

> IT IS UNLIKELY. EARTH IS A SOMEWHAT ORDI-
> NARY PLANET. IF IT HAD NOT BEEN FOR THE
> LAUGHTER, AND FOR YOUR PICTURE, COM-
> PUTER NUT, I PROBABLY WOULD NOT HAVE
> COME AT ALL.

"Would it be all right if I contacted you sometime by computer? Would you answer?"

> IT IS UNLIKELY.

He turned. Mist swirled around his slim form, and for a moment all Kate could see was the white circle of his face.

"Please don't go yet," she said in a rush. "I can't bear for you to leave here feeling like this about Earth . . . about us."

> I MUST. AT THIS VERY MOMENT I SHOULD BE
> ORBITING IOXIA, PREPARING FOR MY ANNUAL

VISIT THERE. ALREADY I HAVE STAYED TOO
LONG. I THOUGHT IT WOULD BE A MATTER OF
MINUTES, THAT I WOULD POP IN, BREAK EV-
ERYBODY UP, AS YOU SAY, AND BE ON MY
WAY. UNFORTUNATELY I WAS NOT AS FUNNY
AS I THOUGHT I WOULD BE.

"Where is this Ioxia?" Kate asked. "How far away?"

OBNOXIA, I SOMETIMES CALL IT TO BE AMUS-
ING. IT IS KNOWN AS THE BAD ODOR PLANET,
WHICH IS PERHAPS WHY I WANTED THE FRESH
CLEAN SOUND OF A GOOD LAUGH RINGING IN
MY EARS TO SEND ME ON MY WAY. WELL,
COMPUTER NUT, GOOD-BYE.

Kate swallowed. "Good-bye, BB-9."

BB-9 stepped into the mist and disappeared. Kate waited.
After a moment the mist opened like a curtain and BB-
9 stepped back into view. He was smiling.

YOU KNOW HOW MANY IOXIANS IT TAKES TO
SMELL UP A PLANET?

Kate waited. BB-9 grinned.

JUST A PHEW.

Suddenly Kate threw back her head and laughed. Her
laughter was genuine, and it surprised her. She could not
remember ever really laughing at a joke before—she

probably never would again—but the joke was a lot more than the smell of the Ioxians.

YOU ARE AMUSED?

Kate nodded. Never having laughed like this before, she reached out to hold onto a tree for support. Her laughter rang through the clearing.

WHY, THANK YOU, COMPUTER NUT,
THANK YOU.

BB-9 smiled at Kate with pleasure.

AND ON THAT ONE—EXCCUUUSSSSE ME!

He turned and once again disappeared into the mist.

Kate stood without moving. She waited, without knowing exactly what she was waiting for. Suddenly she heard thrashing in the bushes behind her. Twigs snapped, leaves tore, branches broke. She spun around.

"Is something there?"

"It's me!"

Willie stumbled into the clearing, gasping for breath. "I've been running after you for miles. I thought I'd never catch up. Where is he?"

"Gone."

"Gone up or just"—he gasped again—"gone?"

"We have to wait here because of the blast-off." Kate looked at him. "You were wonderful, Willie."

"Me? No." He paused for more breath. "I didn't do"—another pause—"anything."

"Yes, you did. We would never have gotten away if it hadn't been for you pointing the wrong way."

"I saw that once"—pause—"in a movie"—gasp—"cowboys."

"Anyway, you saved us."

"Did I miss it?"

"What?"

"The blast-off."

"I don't know."

"I probably did. I miss everything. Like—" He paused, breathed. "Like I come in the TV room and somebody will say, 'Oh, you just missed it,' and I say, 'What?' " Pause, breathe. "And they say, 'A man on *That's Incredible* just swallowed a whole watermelon and—' " Suddenly Willie reached out and grabbed her arm. "Did you see that?"

"What?"

"That light. There. In the sky."

"I don't know. Isn't that just some lights from the city, some sort of reflection from the fog?"

"Not what I saw. It was like something streaking skyward. It was . . ." He took one long, shuddering breath. "BB-9."

They waited, staring together up into the sky. "I wish," Willie said, "BB-9 had stayed longer, at least long enough to tell us why ambulances on Exxyor have square wheels, don't you?"

Kate nodded.

"And why nurses on Plotovia wear pointed hats."

"Maybe," Kate said, "they have pointed heads."

"That could well be," Willie said, and as if on some mutual signal, they turned and started for home.

Kate walked into the kitchen and threw back the hood of her jacket. Drops of water sprinkled the floor.

Cassie was slumped at the table. Around her were the remains of the party—busted balloons, torn hats, wet napkins, spilled cake.

"How did it go?" Kate asked.

"Can't you see? It was a nightmare," Cassie answered. "Minna's poodle got so nervous with Heidi slobbering on her that she wet all over the house. I had to follow her around, dropping paper napkins on her puddles. One puddle took thirteen paper napkins. Thirteen!"

"That's too bad."

"And then Dad comes up and says that you have an alien in the basement and for us to come down, and we go to the basement door to see the alien, and all of a sudden Heidi goes wild, absolutely wild. It was like she was on the scent of something. She ran down the steps and started scratching at the garage door, and she's got long toenails—did you see her toenails?"

Kate shook her head.

"Well, she left big scratches in the door, *big* scratches, that deep. Dad's furious. He said I can never have dogs over again. He said, 'Cassandra—' You know how he sounds when he's really serious. 'Cassandra, you are never to invite dogs to this house again.' Can you believe that?"

Kate smiled.

"Well, you must be feeling better," Cassie said. "You're smiling like yourself again."

"I feel better than myself."

"I wish I did. I mean, I have been worried about you for two weeks, really worried, and now here you are, going to Burger's with Willie, having aliens in the basement. Now I'm the one who's miserable. No date for the pep rally, and tomorrow I have to fill in Heidi's scratch marks with plastic wood."

Laughing, Kate turned and went down the hall and into her room. She opened the curtains.

Outside, the fog was breaking up. In an opening patch of sky, she could see a single star. She made a small sound, almost a sigh, and watched until it was out of sight.

On to Cabrigilio

Kate threw open the door of the office. The patients waiting to see her father looked up from their magazines. She ran to the desk.

"Dad said I got a message on the computer yesterday." She was gasping for breath. She had run all the way from school. "And he forgot to bring it home. He didn't even tell me until this morning. Can you believe that? Something as vital as a computer message!"

"I have it right here."

Miss Markham opened her desk drawer and pulled out a sheet of paper.

"Is it from who I think it is?"

"Yes, it's from your space person, only next time please tell him not to interrupt when I'm doing the bills. It's very distracting."

"I will." Kate took the sheet of paper. Standing in the office with a smile on her face, she read:

> GREETINGS, COMPUTER NUT. YOU SEE THAT I
> DECIDED TO CONTACT YOU AFTER ALL. I AM
> NOW LEAVING IOXIA. IT WAS WORSE THAN
> USUAL THIS TIME, CAUSING ME TO THINK AN
> AMUSING THOUGHT.
> WHAT IS WORSE THAN SMELLING AN IOXIAN?
> SMELLING TWO IOXIANS.
> ELMER SAID, "HA-HA," AND I HOPE YOU DO
> TOO. FROM TIME TO TIME, WHEN I HAVE AN
> AMUSING THOUGHT, I WILL CONTACT YOU
> AND SHARE IT. EVEN IF I CANNOT HEAR YOU
> LAUGH IN PERSON, I HAVE THE ABILITY TO RE-
> PLAY YOUR LAUGHTER IN MY MIND AND SO
> WILL HAVE IT WITH ME ALWAYS. MY NEXT
> STOP IS THE PLANET CABRIGILIO.
> YOU KNOW WHAT A TWO-HEADED, EIGHT-
> ARMED CABRIGILION MONSTER EATS FOR
> BREAKFAST?
> A-N-Y-BODY HE WANTS.
> OH, YES, WHAT DOES A HUNDRED-POUND
> CABRIGILION CANARY SAY?
> HERE, KITTY, KITTY.

> I COULD GO ON ALL DAY ABOUT CABRIGILIO.
> IT IS THAT KIND OF PLANET. A CABRIGILION
> MONSTER IS PUSHING HER BABY MONSTER IN
> THE PARK.
> A PASSER-BY SAYS, MADAM, YOUR BABY'S
> TEETH ARE LIKE RUSTY NAILS, THE HOLES IN
> HIS NOSE ARE SLIME PITS, HIS EYES ARE
> SMALL RED COALS, AND HIS BREATH IS LIKE
> ROTTEN MANURE.
> THANK YOU, SAYS THE CABRIGILION
> MONSTER.

"Now, don't tell me you think that stuff's funny," Miss Markham said.

Kate glanced up, smiling. She nodded.

"Whoever's sending it must be pretty far out."

"You could say that," Kate admitted.

"Did you ever get to meet this—what did he call himself?"

"BB-9. Yes, I met him."

"And was he as far out as his jokes?"

"Every bit."

Kate turned. Her smile broadened as she finished reading the message. Holding the sheet of paper against her chest, she picked up the phone to call Willie.

> P.S. I TOLD MY ROBOT ELMER ABOUT THE PYR-
> AMIDS YOUR CHEERLEADERS MAKE OF THEM-
> SELVES, AND HE GOT THE OTHER ROBOTS TO

JOIN HIM IN A SIMILAR EFFORT. I DID NOT
HAVE THE HEART TO TELL HIM THEY HAD IT
UPSIDE DOWN. BB-9 LOGGING.

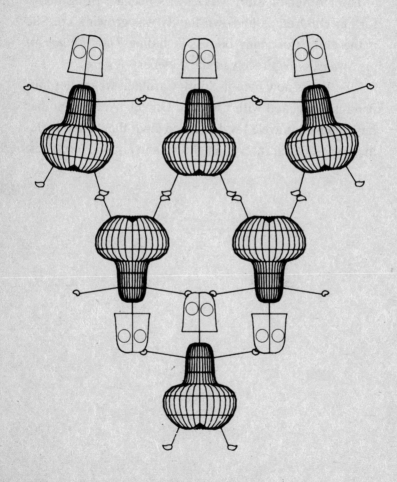

About the Author

Betsy Byars was born in Charlotte, North Carolina, and lived there until her graduation from Queens College.

The mother of four, Mrs. Byars began writing books for her children as her own family was growing up. She is the author of many books, including *The Summer of the Swans*, which received the Newbery Award.

Mrs. Byars now lives in South Carolina, where her husband is associated with Clemson University. She and her husband have traveled widely throughout the United States in pursuit of their interest in gliding and antique airplanes.